NUTTY

By T.M. McCauley

Dedicated to all the homies who gave their life or freedom to the streets of North & North East Portland

T.M. McCauley

Introduction

Nutty is a mind bending story that takes place in pregentrified Portland Oregon. It follows the life of former gangster Latrezz "Nut" Tillman and his struggle to stay legit, stay alive and stay sane. Loosely based on North & North East Portland Gang Culture. This literature is for entertainment purposes only. All characters and events are figments of the author's imagination. Any similarity to any event or person living or dead is purely coincidence. Once again this is for entertainment purposes only. We do not encourage gangbanging or causing harm to people of Aprikan Descent. We do encourage self expression and self presvervation. Intended for mature audiences only. Enjoy!!!

TABLE OF CONTENTS

Chapter 1

Mont and Cliff had altered their Mother's basement into the "Man Cave" of any teen aged, American, black boy's dream. The walls were decorated with posters of beautiful melanated women, black leaders, rappers, scenes from gangster movies, and personal photos that resemebled album covers. On the back wall of the basement hung a wooden Cross that was surrounded by photos of Black Jesus and obituraries. The opposite wall held a 72 inch flat screen T.V. , below it sat an entertainment center with the latest gaming console and a stereo system. The center of the room was furnished with a black couch, matching reclyners and a coffee table. Although they were only 15 and 16, the brothers had managed to furnish their space mainly through hustling and "Jugging" in the streets.

Mont, the elder of the two brothers, sat at the coffee table twisting a blunt. Cliff stood over an ironing board while carefully applying creases to his Levi 501's jeans. The pair was often mistaken for twins. Both stood just about 5'4 or 5'5 with facial features of a pubescent young man. Often the two dressed similar as well, as most members of their gang would also do as a tactic to throw off police or witnesses in case something happened. The main way you could tell the two is apart is that Mont was usually more social and Cliff was usually quiet in group settings.

Mont grinned wide, "All the bitches gon' be in there tonight. I wanna take Cookie fine ass down so bad!"

Cliff, looked up at Mont "Don't she fuck with the Alberta nigga... uh JR?"

Mont jumped up, "Yea that's why I want to fuck her. Fuck that bitch ass nigga and his dead homies!"

"He supposed to had dumped on L and them last summer," Cliff added. Cliff was aware his brother had already knew about the incident, he mainly said it to see what Mont's intentions were.

"Well if he in there tonight he's goin' to definately feel our presence!" Mont replied.

Cliff picked his pants up off the ironing board. "You always tryin' to start some shit. I'm tryin to knock a bitch mayne," Cliff popped his collar, "On the set!"

Retha cracked the basement door and called out "Mont!"

Mont jumped up almost spilling the plate of weed that was on his lap. "What's up?" he called back.

Retha put a hand on her hip, "Y'all better not be down there smokin! Its dinner in the oven." Her tone softened. "Cifford baby,"

"Yes Mama," Cliff replied.

"Don't let your brother get you in no shit you hear me," She knew her son too well.

Mont smacked his teeth. "Mom you know I aint gon let nothin happen to my little bro."

Retha sighed, "Alright I'm headed to work. Y'all don't be out too late.

"Okay Mama" Cliff replied.

Mont and Cliff bailed down the street, both wearing black beenies, hoodies and Chuck Taylors. They stopped when they spotted another teenager also wearing all black Converse, hoody and beanie. Nacho had been friends with the Tillman's since elementary. His real name was Darius but everyone called him Nacho because he was half Chicano.

"What's up y'all," Nacho greeted the duo with handshakes and head nods.

"What's up with my nigga! What that Killingsworth like?" Mont replied.

and deep dimples, as she reached out to hug Mont. "Hey Lamont! How you been?"

"I been alright. Who you in here with?" Mont asked.

"You remember my Cousin Erica? I rode with her." Cookie replied pointing in the direction of her cousin.

Mont didn't really care who she rode with unless it was her man JR. He let his guard down a little and leaned back to her ear. "Damn girl you country now!"

"Shut up! Why does everybody say that, I am not country!" she said as she giggled, cheesing ear to ear. Her southern drawl was very strong and another reason why Mont, JR and alot of other young men wanted her.

Mont continued, unknowingly rubbing his hands.,"I see Oklahoma done made a beautiful young woman out of you though."

Cookie blushed. "Well thank you Lamont. You turned out to be a handsome young man yourself."

"Maybe we can kick it sometime?" Mont suggested.

"I got a man so I don't know about that." Cookie said still blushing.

"I've been knowing you since first grade Cookie, you know I would never disrespect you," Mont innocently grinned, although deep down he was already wondering how long it would take to see her naked.

"Well I guess maybe we can catch up sometime. Here put your number in my phone." Cookie held her phone out. Mont took the phone and put his number in it.

"What that Murda Gang like nigga!" A voice yelled from out the crowd. Mont looked up with the phone still in his hand making eye contact with JR. Mont grinned then handed Cookie her phone back before giving her one last hug. JR's face turned to a cold sneer as Mont started back toward his friends.

"A all the Alberta niggas just walked in," Stomp said nervously.

"Well what y'all tryin to do?" Nacho asked.

"Fuck them brand ass niggas. Its whatever!" Mont cut in.

Across the room JR approached Cookie. "You just gon' disrespect me like that bitch?!"

"Excuse me? Why are you talkin to me like that baby?" Cookie replied.

"You over here exchangin' numbers with that off brand ass nigga. Fuckin around with my enemies bitch. You tryin' to make me look stupid!?" JR scolded her. His dark beady eyes screamed fury.

"For one I'm not your bitch! And for two I've known Lamont since we were little kids and he knows I'm not the type of girl to cheat on my man." Cookie replied, this time with a little fire in her voice.

JR grabbed Cookie's arm, "Bitch take yo ass home before I get pissed off."

Cookie tried to pull away, "Let go of me! Im not your bitch and I don't have to go anywhere! I don't got time for this shit nigga, you dont have to be with me!"

JR cocked back to hit Cookie, Mont stepped in and viciously pushed JR. "What's up nigga!? Put yo hands on a man though pussy ass nigga!" Mont put his dukes up.

Cookie stepped between them. "No, Mont I can handle myself y'all dont need to be fightin."

In the middle of the party Nacho and one of the Alberta Block teens yelled back and forth. Nacho swiftly knocked the other teen's hat off. Before he could react, Cliff shot from the crowd with a clean blow to the right side of the other young man's face. At that very moment, all hell broke loose as several of the teens in the party started fighting.

Mont reached out and connected with JR's chin. The two exchanged blows until some one yelled out, "Po-Po outside. If you got anything on you run out the back now!" Just about all of the kids who were fighting darted out the back of the house. Just up the block the teens regrouped.

The Killingsworth Gang stood on one corner and Alberta Gang stood on the other.

"Killa Gang you bitch ass niggas!" Stomp yelled out to the other group.

"Y'all can't fuck with the Murder Squad! And Stomp yo' bitch ass for damn sure don't want none homie," JR fired back. He turned to one of his comrades. "A tell Tic and Junee we on the other side." Another teen nodded while giving out directions on his phone.

"Why y'all callin for back up. Get down!" Stomp challenged the other group.

JR walked to the middle of the street. "What's up then catch that fade."

Before anyone could notice Stomp hesitating, Mont met JR in the middle of the street. The two began throwing blows back and forth once again. Stomp stepped in the middle of the street just as a white sedan aggressively pulled up to the group of rowdy teens. Out of the car emerged Tic and Junee. Both men stood over 6'5. They had a good 10 years and 100 pounds on every one else outside.

"What's up nigga!" Junee said as he approached Stomp. Stomp's face froze, he had left his gun in his car and did not know how to get himself out of this situation.

"I'm Baby Stomp!" Stomp roared out.

"So! Fuck you, and Big Stomp!" Junee caught Stomp's chin, dropping him to the ground.

With out saying a single word or drawing any attention to himself, Cliff went into action. BANG! BANG! BANG!. The crowd dispersed. Cliff aimed once more toward Junee as he hustled to get into his car. BANG! BANG! BANG! BANG!

"FUCK!!!" Junee cried out clutching his rear. "Them little bitch ass niggas popped me!"

"Dont even trip Murda Gang we gon' handle that shit though." Tic reassured his comrade. Tic and Junee sped off into the night while the teens on the street scrambled and police cars flooded the corner.

The teens rode in silence for about five minutes. Usually Baby Stomp would have been blasting his music and talking shit, but his nervousness left him alone with his own thoughts. Nacho broke the silence, "You okay bro? That was a big ass nigga that rocked off on you."

Baby Stomp hesitantly replied, "I ain't trippin off that shit. I'm just tryin to make sure we reach our destination with out gettin' pulled over. I knew I should of brought my thang in there. I would've shot that big ass brand nigga in the face!"

Mont cut in "It's cool homie everybody gon take an L. Lil' bro handled that shit though, on the set." Mont looked back at his little brother. "We goin to have to get rid of yo' thang little bro,"

"I already know." Cliff calmly replied. "Man somebody light some dodi up though. I need to calm my nerves.

Nacho pulled out a blunt and lit it up. "Them niggas was weak as fuck. We all the same age and weight class, why'd they have to call in they're big homies like that?"

"Well he got what was comin to him, bullies get popped on Killingsworth Street homie," Mont replied. "If y'all want to, y'all can crash at our crib tonight. Its too hot to be out on the streets."

"I dont know, Momz is goin to be trippin if I don't make it in tonight." Stomp said.

"Nigga you was just talkin about shootin' a nigga in the face and you worried about curfew?" Mont replied displaying a confused facial expression. Monts phone rang. "Hello?"

"Hey, this is Cookie," A sweet voice said on the other end of the phone.

"What's up Cookie? Y'all make it out of there okay?" Mont asked. The other teens grew silent so they could ear hustle.

"Yes. Im fine, I was actually just calling to check on you. And I really appreciate you standing up for me like you did." Cookie replied.

"It's all good baby." Mont replied as smooth as he could. "What y'all about to do now?"

"Erica was tryin' to get somethin to eat, then I dont know probably go home. We picked up her other cousins when all that shooting started so we gotta take them home too."

"Why don't y'all come over to the crib?" Mont suggested.

"I don't know Mont, its kind of late," she responded.

"It's cool, I promise I don't bite. It's just me, my lil bro and a couple of homies." Mont replied.

"Ask him do they have some weed?" Erica asked from the background.

Mont grinned wide, "Tell her we got some bomb."

"Well send me your address. We'll come by," Cookie said.

"Okay, see you in a minute." Mont said then hung up his phone, cheesing ear to ear. "Hell yea!"

"How you know she aint tryin to set us up for them bitch ass niggas?!" Stomp asked.

"I don't think she like that, and if that's the case my house is the last place they want to bring their issue." Mont assured his friends.

"I'm down homie, but I feel where Stomp comin' from too though, cant let our guard down." Nacho replied.

"Don't trip homie." Mont reassured his friends. "Y'all act like y'all scared of pussy or somethin,"

"I probably fucked more bitches than you know!" Stomp spoke up, finally relaxing at the thought of being in the presence of a couple soft legs. The whole group erupted in laughter.

After bending just a few more corners, Stomp's car parked in the alley behind the TIllmans' home. The boys had just enough time to get into the basement and pull out some liquor and weed before Mont's phone began to ring. Mont stopped what he was doing and anxiously answered; "Hello,"

"Hey, where can I park?" Cookie asked.

"Pull right in front" Mont replied. "I'll come let y'all in."

"Damn! Do one of y'all have an extra shirt I can get?" Stomp asked. He didn't need to explain why, his clothes showed evidence of the cold hard rain drenched concrete he found himself on after the altercation just 90 minutes prior.

"I got a big ass pack of Tee's in that closet. Shit I'm about to grab one too," Mont replied. All the teens quickly put on the fresh t-shirts and placed the others in a trash bucket in the corner of the room. Mont headed up the stairs.

When Mont reached the porch, Cookie's group was just stepping out of Erica's car. Although Cookie was by far the most attractive of all the young women, Mont couldn't help but to admire her company as well. Erica was brown skinned and thick, and when she walked her hips swayed side to side like a prissy cat. Their cousins, Misty and Nicole, were both caramel complexioned and petite with perky breasts and smooth legs. The sisters weren't as thick as their cousins, but were both pretty enough to be models or actresses.

Inside the teens parlayed all night listening to music and playing cards. Cookie thought to herself, Mont and Cliff must have an endless supply of weed. Once one blunt went out another was quickly set ablaze. She didn't smoke much but would occasionally take a toke of the sweet smelling reefer being passed around. "I don't think I've ever been this high y'all," Cookie said to no one in particular.

"Well slow down baby, aint no rushin to the moon." Mont said.

Cookie giggled. "I for damn sure aint rushin nowhere

no time soon,"

"Y'all don't have no bomb like this out in Oklahoma huh?" Nacho asked.

"Nah, you right about that." Cookie replied.

The sounds from the stereo changed to a smooth R&B song. Erica jumped up and turned up the volume. "Ooh! This is my song right here!" She said as she started dancing. "Y'all dance with me so I'm not up here lookin like a fool," She summoned her cousins with her hands.

"I'll dance with you," Nacho cut in, taking his chance to put his bid in with Erica. Nacho and Erica started casually dancing and laughing. At that moment the young men all made brief eye contact, it was a verbal communication understood all across teenaged black America. The boys knew it was time to make their moves.

"What's up Misty and Nicole, come play us in these cards, "Stomp called out to the sisters as he mixed cards.

"Y'all niggas aint tired of gettin y'alls asses whooped in spades yet?" Misty replied sarcastically.

"Well since you wanna talk shit, lets play a different game." Stomp replied grinning.

Nicole turned her head toward Stomp. "What game?"

"A little somethin my pasty patna showed me. Its called Presidents and Assholes." Stomp replied. "I can show y'all how to play." Stomp broke down the drinking game to the young ladies as they sat at the table.

Mont slid next to Cookie on the sofa. "So what's up country girl?"

Cookie giggled. "Why you always tryin to call somebody country?"

"I know its goin to make you giggle and I get to see them dimples come out." Mont smoothly replied as Cookie blushed, "That country shit don't bother me."

"You be tryin to be all tough but you're really very sweet." Cookie said in a soft tone. "And even though I asked you not too, I really appreciate you standin up for me

Lamont. You know how to make a girl feel secure." She grinned at Mont.

"Well that's what a man supposed to do, not put his hands on you." Mont replied. Although he knew it wasn't the way a true player should operate, he couldn't help but to throw shade at his rival JR.

"After that I'm done with him. All he wants to do all day is talk to me like he's crazy and get drunk." Cookie looked up to see if Mont was tuned in. "Then he keeps tryin to pressure me to fuck him. The other day he got mad and slammed my door."

"Y'all ain't never did nothin?" Mont replied, surprised that a girl from North East Portland wasn't having sex.

"We've like kissed and I let him suck my titties but that's it. He begged to go down on me, so I finally let him about a week ago and ever since that he's been mad at me because I wasn't ready to give him none."

"Damn," Mont accidentally said out loud.

"What?" Cookie asked. "We only been together two months. Shit I ain't even give my last boyfriend none and we was together almost a year before I moved back."

"Are you a virgin?" Mont asked.

Cookie began to blush. "Yes, I've just never felt comfortable enough to go there with anybody. And plus I don't got time to be gettin' pregnant!"

In most cases, Mont would never believe these words coming from a girl in his neighborhood. For some odd reason though he knew she was telling the truth. She was just too innocent. At that moment he knew he would have to be with her to get what so many like him lusted for.

"That's cool though. I think I need a girl like you on my side," Mont said as he looked in Cookies eyes. She leaned over and kissed him on the lips. The others saw but were too busy entertaining each other to say anything. The rest of the night Mont and Cookie sat cuddled up, cupcaking on the sofa. Mont knew that later his peers would tease him about being so tender with her. He didn't really care though, at that exact moment she was his. She needed him to feel more secure and he needed her to give him what every gangster needs; a woman's love.

Chapter 2

Tic violently sped through the rain soaked streets. Junee, in the passenger seat, was sweating profusely. "FUCK!!! Fresh out the can and already in some shit. I'm ready to tear some shit up." Tic and Junee had both been released from Sheridan Correctional Facility earlier that week. They had both pulled 100 Month bids for a string of robberies they were involved in. They, along with some of their other comrades spent a whole summer ripping off drug dealers as far south as Eugene and as far North as Spokane. While incarcerated the massive duo had earned a reputation behind their skill with their hands. They had only anticipated opening up a couple cans of whoop ass when they first got word from one of their little homies that it was a royal rumble at the party.

"Don't trip Murda Gang, believe this shit gon' get handled." Tic reassured his friend. "This shit for life with me homie its on sight."

"We might end up right back in that mothafucka but thats better than lettin' em lay me down. R.I.P. Baby Noodle!" Junee was more thinking out loud than he was replying to Tic.

"I wasn't even from the hood yet when that shit happened. That nigga Taz bitch ass slid through trippin." Tic's expression turned cold as his mind traveled to a place both nostalgic and traumatic at the same time. A tear slowly rolled out of Tic's eye. Even though it had been twelve years since he witnessed his childhood friend's brutal murder, he could still feel the warm blood on his face and hands. Before that incident Tic had been into sports and Church. That night he was mixed into Alberta Block, 9 months later he found himself taking his first mugshot.

As Tic turned on to Vancouver street his phone began to ring. "What's up?!"

"Where y'all at? JR told me the lil' niggas popped Junee." On the other end of the line was One Shot. He had earned that name based on his accuracy with a pistol.

One Shot stood about 5'11 with a slim build and a cold expression that never seemed to leave his face. Even when smiling, the stone cold look in his eyes was unforgiving and promised lethal repercussions to anyone who crossed him.

"Yea, them little niggas didn't want to see us though." Junee replied.

"Yall aint on the yard no more, these little niggas will kill you," One Shot lectured.

"I feel you big cuddin. I'm ready to handle this shit though. Im sittin kind of light though." Tic said as he pulled into the parking lot of Emanuel Hospital.

"Don't trip I got somethin for you." One Shot responded in a calm tone.

"When can I come through?" Tic anxiously asked.

"Im on yo' bumper nigga! Look in yo rear view." At that moment Tic looked in his mirror. A green Subaru with two bikes on its hood slowly crept into the parking lot then blinked its brights twice.

Tic stopped in front of the emergency entrance and hopped out. He half dragged Junee into the front lobby. At the sight of the two massive men struggling to get in the door, the nurses immediately scrambled for a stretcher. After finally loading Junee on to the stretcher, Tic turned to one of the nurses, "Hey, can you make sure I can get back there? I'm going to move my car."

"No problem." The young chubby white nurse replied in a bubbly voice.

At that exact moment, just three and a half miles away from Emanuel Hospital, Taz' house was filled with the tunes of Johnny Guitar Watson. He looked up at his woman, Kisha, and couldn't be more pleased. She was an old school kind of fine with coffee brown skin, full lips and bedroom eyes that she cut at Taz with every moan. He laid still in a trance llike state watching her big brown titties bounce up and down in a circular like motion.

"FUCK!!!" Kisha cried out as she climbed off of Taz. "I

can't go no more Daddy I'm exhausted."

Taz wiped sweat from his brow with a confused expression on his face. "What you mean baby we can"t stop now."

"I'm sorry Daddy," Kisha said as she dropped to the bed.

"You aint 'bout to have me with the blue balls!"

Taz' real name was Tasir Tillman, but what made the nickname "Taz" stick was his resemblance to the cartoon character "Tasmanian Devil". Ever since elementary he was short and stocky, and when it was time to get physical he moved like a tornado, causing havoc and destruction to anyone or anything in his path. With that same animal like movement, Kisha felt her hips being pulled into the tornado.

She loved when Taz got riled up and handled her like this. She let out a moan as she imagined how it would be if King Kong ever got the little white girl in bed. It only took about 3 minutes of admiring the way his woman's plump round ass jiggled with every thrust.

"AAAWWWW!!!!" He felt himself explode and fell limp for about 10 minutes. He felt as weak as if he had died. It was the obnoxious ringing of his phone that woke Taz out of his hibernation like state.

"Who the fuck callin you this late?" Kisha snapped.

"I dont know, probably one of the homies." Taz picked up his phone and looked at the name on the screen. Sure enough it was his homie Black. "What's up nigga? Everything cool?"

"Its always cool with the Killa Gang, heard yo' nephews left the brand niggas lickin' their wounds though." Black replied.

"Damn I aint heard shit." Taz straightened up, "Let me tap in with them little niggas. I'm going to hit you right back."

"Yep" Black responded.

Back at Mont and Cliff's place all of the teens were sprawled out, exhausted from all the weed and liquor they had consumed. Mont hadn't noticed that his phone went dead about an hour ago. It was now close to 5 a.m. and Retha would be home by dawn.

Meanwhile Taz felt a short lived relief when he heard his nephew's voice come over the phone "Hello,"

"What's up?" Taz asked in a husky voice.

"Hold on, Hold on. A y'all turn that shit down! Okay can you hear me now?" Mont's voice asked.

"Yea-" Before Taz could let the words out his mouth Mont cut back in.

"Well any way I aint here right now you've reached my voice mail. To the beep," Taz angrily sneered at his phone as he realized he'd reached his immature nephew's obnoxious voice mail again. Next he called Cliff's phone. Still no luck. On the other end of the line Cliff's phone was set to silent mode so he wasn't aware of the three missed calls from his uncle.

Once Taz realized he wouldn't reach them by phone he decided he would just go to see them. Within two minutes he was dressed. "Is everything okay baby? Where you goin?" Kisha asked.

Taz tucked his nickel plated chrome .357 into his pocket. "Its all good baby. I just gotta go check on my folks real quick."

"Okay well dont be too long baby," Kisha pleaded. She was well aware of the lifestyle her man led but she still worried at times like this when he would go out in the middle of the night to deal with streets.

As Taz cruised the back streets toward his sister's house he couldn't help but reflect on the example that he had set for his nephews. As teenagers, he and his little brother made a career out of putting in work, hustling and "thuggin" in general. Sometimes he wished his nephews would go their own route and be like some of those square kids he saw going to work after school. He quickly put that thought out of his head, deep down he knew that the boys couldn't help but want to participate in the lifestyle that brought him so much glory and pain.

Just as Taz stepped to the front door of Retha's house, her car slowly pulled into the driveway. Taz was hoping he would beat her there, she loved her little brother to death and loved the close relationship he kept with her sons but also knew he was a bad influence. Retha stepped out of her car and put her hands on her hips.

"What's up Sis?" Taz innocently asked.

"What's up my ass. Taz you know damn well you don't get up this early. What the hell goin on?" She asked in an inculpating voice.

"I knew you was goin' to be off around this time and thought maybe I'd treat my favorite sister to some breakfast, damn!" He lied through his teeth.

"I'm ya' only sister nigga so save them lies for ya' woman. The last time I seen you at my house this early you and Nut was about to go on the run." She knew her brother well, and if he was up this early something was going on.

"For real sis. I was thinkin maybe we can hit the Overlook or somethin, my treat." Taz pleaded.

"You full of shit!" Retha said as she opened her door and stepped in. Taz followed behind her just as he did when they were kids. "Damn them little mothafuckas got my whole house smellin' like weed." Retha said as she opened a window.

"I'll go wake them up for you," Taz started toward the basement.

"You probably smoked it with they little asses. What you goin tell 'em" Retha sarcastically replied.

"Damn Sis, why you so hard on yo lil bro?" Taz asked bemusedly as he started down the stairs casually. He knew Retha was right, he didn't care if the boys were smoking because he often smoked with them.

Taz had cultured his nephews on all the tricks and trades of the street, from hustling to gambling and even how to pull a successful stick up. What he really wanted was to see what happened last night, before his sister got downstairs. "God damn, Y'all little niggas had it crackin' in this mothafucka last night huh." Taz stated as he stepped in the room filled with teens sprawled across the floor and couches, next to empty bottles and ashtrays.

Cliff jumped up, startled by his uncle's raspy voice. "What you doin' here this early Unk? How you get in?"

"Ya' Mama let me in little nigga." Taz replied. All the teens began chuckling groggily between yawns. "I aint playin, y'all might want to clean this shit up before she get down here. I been callin y'all little asses all mornin'. Get up and get ya shit together I need to holla at y'all once your company bounce." The young women in the room looked around at each other confused, not really sure what the stocky man in front of them had to say that was so important.

"Well I guess it is time we get goin'. We didn't mean no disrespect we was just havin a good time." Cookie spoke up. Taz thought to himself what he would do to the sweet sounding country girl if she was old enough.

"That's okay baby girl, just don't let these knuckle heads get yo' pretty self in no trouble you hear." Cookie giggled at Taz' all of a sudden sweet demeanor.

"Oh hell naw!" Retha came stomping down the stairs. Even when upset, her pretty round face showed evidence of the ravishing young woman she once was. "I know damn well y'all aint got the nerve to have company in my house lookin' like this. Actin a damn fool smokin' and drinkin'!"

Taz motioned toward his sister. "Damn sis' don't embarass the boys. You should be happy they're hangin' with such lovely young ladies. Now don't scare the girls off."

"Last time I checked I paid the bills in here, in a minute I'm 'bout to embarass yo' ass with these hands if you keep tellin me what to do." Retha said in a fiesty voice twisting her face. The kids couldn't help but to chuckle under their breath.

"Damn sis' you know I don't want that issue." Taz held his hands up. "I'll talk to the boys and make sure they get it cleaned up down here. You just go get ready so we can catch the buffet."

"All this shit better be cleaned up by the time I get back. And Taz hurry yo fat ass up." Retha snapped then turned on her heels and stormed upstairs.

"Alright I need to holla at y'all over here in the back real quick." Taz ordered realizing this was his chance to figure out what happened the night before. The young men followed behind Taz to the laundry room.

"A y'all lets straighten up just a little bit for them, their Mom was kind of upset by the way we left this place." Cookie suggested to her cousins. The young women began slowly making the basement tidy again.

Once all of the boys were in the laundry room with the door shut, Taz began to interview them. "So what's up? What happened last night?"

Mont spoke up, "We had got into it with them fools at the party, then a couple of their big homie's hopped out. Them niggas was like 6'7 or 6'8 Unk. One of 'em rocked off on Baby Stomp so lil' bro' tore his ass up."

Taz turned toward Baby Stomp. He couldn't help but notice the resemblance the young man had to his father. However, he wasn't sure just how much of his father had rubbed off on him since he'd been incarcerated for the past eight years. "You okay little cuddin'?"

Baby Stomp was anxious to be apart of the conversation, "I'm cool big homie. The bitch ass nigga caught me with out the thang."

"Don't sweat it homie. If you take enough fades, everybody gon' lose a few. The important thing is y'all made it out safe." Taz surveyed the four young men looking at him the same way athletes look to their coach during an intense huddle. "Cliff, did you get rid of the thang yet?"

Cliff shook his head. "Didn't really have time to just yet Unk,"

"Okay, y'all go drop it off around the corner to Black. It's hella early so shouldn't nobody be up to see y'all. Just drop the shit off and get back home." Taz ordered.

"Alright big homie," Nacho replied, confirming he understood the task ahead of him and his homeboys.

"On some real shit though, next time some shit pop off, call ya' uncle immediately. You got to handle business before you get to partyin'," Taz said with a slight grin on his face.

"Taz hurry the hell up before I change my mind!" Retha yelled down the stairs.

"Damn I'm comin," Taz yelled back up the stairs as the teens chuckled.

"Well I guess we goin' to get goin' y'all," Cookie said as the young men came out the back room.

"Alright we'll be in touch," Nacho said as looked toward Erica rubbing his hands, making her blush.

As the teens went up the stairs Mont and Cookie lingered behind. "I really enjoyed your company last night Lamont. Call me when you get a chance." Cookie's mouth made the sound but her eyes did most of the talking.

"I'm goin' to call you later on today," Mont said grinning ear to ear. Cookie puckered her lips up toward Mont's face and the two shared a brief kiss before departing ways. He was excited about his new lady friend but knew it was time to get back to business.

Taz and Retha were the first to leave. Taz began on his way to The Overlook. After bending a couple of corners Retha's phone began to ring. "Hey mama,"

"What you doin baby?" Mrs. Tillman said from the other end of the line.

"Just about to go eat with Taz, he said he gon' take

me to the buffet," Retha cut her eyes at her baby brother. At this moment he realized that The Overlook didn't have a buffet and knew his sister was toying with him.

"Oh, I was goin' to ask you to drive me to the casino baby. They're havin' a big bingo tournament today, and its still early enough to make it." Mrs. Tillman said. Everybody knew for the most part the loveable Grandmother didn't do much but she loved going to the casinos atleast once a week. Gambling was a hobby shared amongst most of those in her family. She didn't realize it but it was the many card games at her house and her brothers back yard dice games that had turned her sons onto gambling in the street.

"Yea we'll take you Mama. We should be there shortly." Retha put her phone back in her lap. "Go get Mama, we about to take her to the casino."

"Who said I was drivin' two hours to the casino?!" Taz asked in a surprised voice.

"I said nigga! It aint like you got to go to work or nothin' fool. So light that little swap weed you got and put the pedal to the metal until we at Mom's!" Retha snapped at her brother.

Taz had to literally bite his tongue so that he wouldn't disrespect his sister. Her sons were beginning to remind her more and more of her brothers. She took most of her frustration out on Taz because he was still active in the streets. Latrezz on the other hand had been trying to go straight ever since he beat his last case the year prior.

"Let me call Kisha to see if she tryin' to go. Damn!" Taz spoke up. It wasn't that he disliked the casino, he just hated when his sister tried to punk him like this. More importantly, he didn't want to put too much distance between himself and his nephews at a time like this. She knew he didn't want to go far from the boys as well but didn't understand why at that moment. She was hoping he would tell her and then turn around. Instead he continued on his way to get his mother, his woman and then to the casino.

As soon as Baby Stomp's car pulled in front of Black's house the front door was swinging open. Black stood there in khaki shorts, a white tank top and black cordoroide house shoes. He motioned the boys to hurry up. Once inside they followed him downstairs to the basement.

"Okay where the thang at?" Black asked. His eye's seemed to glow in the dimly lit room. He was one of the darkest men most people had ever seen. He had tattoos on both arms but one would almost need a flashlight to find them.

Cliff pulled his black .25 out and placed it on the table. Black closely examined it then removed the clip and checked to make sure the chamber was empty. "How many y'all need nephew? This the only dirty one?" Black asked.

"Everybody else had left their shit in the car. I'm the only one who had my thang on me." Cliff responded.

"You little quiet as killa boy! That's how Nut was back in the day. It's always the ones who don't say much and be in the background that be ready to tear some shit up." Black erupted in laughter. He was expecting for Mont or Nacho to be the trigger man. "Hold on I'll be right back."

Black re-entered the room and placed a chrome snub nosed .380 on the table. It was the prettiest gun that Cliff had ever seen and reminded him of something off of a movie. "How many it hold?" Cliff asked while examining his new tool.

"Seven plus one," Black responded. "That mothafucka small but it got some kick to it."

"Naw this shit cool. I can easily conceal it that's all I need." Cliff said as he placed the small pistol in his pocket.

"I got the word on them niggas that hopped out on y'all though. They just touched down from Sheridan. We pressin' the issue on sight!" Black reassured his little homies.

"Who was them fools?" Nacho asked with his arms folded.

"The one that got popped they call him Junee. He used to play football at Lincoln back in the day. I could've swore he had a scholarship to play for U of O, then one day this fool was on the news for some 2-11's. The other cat's name is Tic. Nut pistol whipped his big ass back in the day." Black chuckled as he pictured Tic's lumpy face.

"I'm ready to get on these niggas right now!" Mont exclaimed. Baby Stomp felt his stomach tighten. At this moment he prayed to himself that Black reinforced what Taz said.

"You little crazy Killingsworth ass nigga! Didn't yo' uncle say to kick back for a minute." Black replied. Baby Stomp relaxed as those word's filled him with relief. "I know these niggas, they're my age. Y'all just babies let the G's handle it."

"I'm with the shit though." Mont cut back in.

"I know you got heart little homie. It aint about that though. Y'all hot right now. Ain't no tellin who all seen y'all or what people assumin', Just chill for a second." Black put the situation in perspective for his young homies. He knew that they would show up if he needed, but he refused to send them on a dummy mission.

"That's solid big homie." Nacho said calmly.

"I got somethin' for y'all though." Black pulled a plastic grocery bag out of a nearby cabinet. He dumped the bag out on the table, four sandwich bags of weed fell out. "That's a zip for each of y'all. Do what you want with it."

All the teens grinned ear to ear. "Killingsworth shit!" Baby Stomp exclaimed.

Chapter 3

Meanwhile at the casino, Taz carefully selected a black jack table to sit at. He figured since he was here, he might as well get some money. it only took about seven hands to turn the $100 he put onto the table into $1650. He enjoyed the irritated look on the card dealer's face as he pushed all his red and white chips to the middle of the table and said "Color me up please." The elderly dealer looked as if he had been dealing cards for at least 50 years, and when he was faced the task of tallying all of the young black man's chips he turned red all over. Taz chuckled as he walked away from the table with his winnings.

Taz made his way to the buffet located in the middle of the casino. When he found the table his party was already seated. Kisha had already made him a plate so he didn't need to get up. As he ate, the women at the table carried on with chit chat about gossip and different hair products they liked to use. Mrs. Tillman carefully filled out a Keno slip.

"So Tasir when is you and Kisha goin' to get married and give me some grand babies?" Mrs. Tillman asked causing Kisha to blush.

"We workin on it Mama. I just need a little time to get a few things in order is all." Taz replied.

"The only thing you need is the Lord's blessing. All that other stuff y'all can go through together. That's the point of being married. Have a partner. Before your Daddy passed it was always us against the world. Trust me, that woman will make you stronger son." Mrs. Tillman said as she caught Kisha's eye. Kisha cheesed back at her potential future mother in law.

"Taz sorry ass aint tryin to marry nobody," Retha couldn't help but to cut in.

"When the last time you heard from the boys' daddy? Last I checked me and Latrezz was raisin' them boys." Taz snapped back. What he said had truly hurt Retha's feelings, but she knew deep down that she had brought it on herself.

"Now y'all cut that shit out. Retha you need to stop being so hard on your brother. Now he aint perfect but neither are you. Y'all need to support each other. Family is all we got." Mrs. Tillman pleaded with her children. At that moment, the television on the wall cut to a breaking news story. The headline read, "Man hospitalized after gang related shooting."

Taz's eyes got big as he studied the television. The women at the table didn't miss his interest in the story. Mrs. Tillman spoke up. "That's a damn shame. Retha you need to be thankful that your boys ain't into all that bullshit. Taz could be havin them like he was but he aint."

"Right," Retha rolled her eyes at Taz. She was well aware of how much her son's, Mont especially, idolized Taz and knew that they were hanging with the new generation of Killingsworth Street. What she didn't know was her sons had a reputation of their own and often times acted with out their uncles' help or guidance.

Back on the North East side, It was just after noon when Nacho found himself entering Mont and Cliff's basement again. The teens sat around playing video games, smoking weed and discussing the events that took place over the last 24 hours. Having a little action really amused them. Cliff thought to himself about the possibility of going to jail for a Measure 11. He remembered how sick he felt when his uncle Latrezz was on trial and had to spend 18 months in the county. He thought about calling his uncle but didn't want to dissapoint him. Ever since he was acquitted, Latrezz had turned a new leaf. He was working full time, going to school and staying out the way.

"A what's up with Nut?" Nacho asked. "I ain't seen him in a minute,"

"Unk tryin' to stay out the can. He just dodged forty-seven years cuddin." Cliff replied.

"I feel him, that was some crazy shit." Nacho said as he tapped buttons on the game controller.

"Yea them niggas is lucky he not still active." Mont said calmly. He didn't need to elaborate, everyone who knew Nut intimately knew he could be just that at times. On the flip side, Latrezz was very calm and logical. "Shit if I ever dodge a case I'm comin out still active though! I can't picture myself not being active the streets. On the set though." Mont spoke truthfully.

The boys sat around and played videos games until late in the afternoon. This was one of the few activities of leisure that allowed them to be kids. Cliff jumped up out of his seat excited about a play on the video game. "We runnin' back kicks and all type of shit on yo' scrub ass team!"

Mont smacked his teeth. "Man are you playin with them created players again?"

"They're not created. I played with him on the college game and drafted him on when he was ready. All of his stats are realistic." Cliff defended himself.

"Is the nigga a real person? Where can I get a "Cliff DaGiant" jersey from?" Mont asked sounding irritated.

"That do sound like some created shit though cuddin," Nacho chimed between chuckles.

"Fuck y'all. Y'all could've did the same thing. We all in the same league online, y'all just chose not to draft y'all wack ass players." Cliff spoke up.

"Whatever nigga. I'm just sayin, see me with a regular team fool." Mont snapped.

"Here you go. Just accept this L!" Mont taunted his brother.

Nacho laughed hysterically. "Y'all some fools bro."

Mont's phone began to ring. He pulled it out of his pocket and placed it to his ear. "What's up pretty girl?" Cliff and Nacho grew quiet so they could ear hustle. "I aint doin' nothin', just over here spankin' these fools in this game." Mont grinned toward his brother.

"That nigga over there sellin' wolf tickets." Cliff joked.

On the other end of the line Cookie sat on her bed painting her toe nails. "I was just wondering if maybe you wanted to come visit me."

"I would love to come kick it with you as long as yo' Pops aint trippin," Mont didn't really care about her father. He was hoping she would change her mind so he could lay low while the heat was on. On the other hand he really wanted a bite of that sweet Cookie.

"My Mom and Dad went out of town for the weekend." Cookie bit her lip. "If you come over I'll cook for you and we can watch movies. Please Mont! I be gettin' scared in this house all alone."

"What you got to be scared of?!" Mont asked trying to stall.

"Aww shit this nigga about to go eat the groceries." Cliff said to Nacho as they began chuckling. Mont flipped his middle finger at his brother and friend.

"I always be hearin' these creepy sounds and ever since I moved here I keep havin these crazy nightmares." Cookie's voice resembled a frightened little girl. Mont broke out laughing. "I knew I should of kept that too myself. You probably think I'm a baby. I'm so embarrassed." Mont could feel her blushing through the phone.

"I didn't mean no harm baby. I thought you was playin'." Mont had to avoid eye contact with Nacho and Cliff to keep a straight face. "I'll come keep you safe. Where you live?"

"I stay on 12th & Stanton, on the other side of Irving Park." Cookie replied sweetly.

"Oh y'all over there with the rich people. What Pops doin' out of town anyway? Sellin' dope?" Mont asked playfully.

"No fool." Cookie giggled. "He just works hard and trusts in GOD."

"Right. Well shit give me a little minute and I'll make my way over there." Mont said calmly.

"Okay, see you soon." Cookie said then hung the phone up. She didn't really know what to expect from Mont but she knew she wanted to be in his presence.

"Nigga you heard uncle Taz. We got to keep it cool for a minute. We can't be out here slippin' tryin to get some pussy." Cliff spoke up. Mont knew his little brother was right but at the end of the day he was still a 16 year old boy with raging hormones.

"The Killa Gang don't never slip nigga!" Mont snapped.

"Yea well you actin like a mark right now fool. Brown nosin and shit huh." Cliff taunted his big brother as he casually turned to walk away. Mont swiftly scooped his brother off of his feet and slammed him onto the sofa.

"Nigga respect yo' elders! I'm big bro' in this muthafucka!" Mont declared.

Cliff reached up to counter his elder brother. "Only by 13 months fool!" Mont dug his knuckles into Cliff's ribs. "Ahhh" Cliff cried out. Nacho sat back and laughed. He had known the Tillmans long enough to know that they would never really hurt each other so it was best just to let the brother's scuffle.

"Stay on yo' toes though little North East Sida." Mont said as his brother fought to get free. "Okay I'm about to let you up. You done yet?" Mont and Cliff both panted heavily. Cliff nodded. Mont dropped a WWF style elbow on Cliff then shoved him away.

"Y'all got to be the craziest niggas I know!" Nacho said as he chuckled. The brothers dusted themselves off.

"Well shit if you goin', I'll walk with you over there to make sure you cool." Cliff spoke up.

"It's good, she stay in the Irving District. Ain't nobody over there." Mont replied.

"How you goin' to get over there though? You could take the bike and ride the back streets but then you goin' to be sweaty when you get there. Or you could take the bus which means you takin' the 72 to the 6 or the 8 and you damn sure goin' to see somebody on Tri-Met." Cliff elaborated on what he meant when he told his brother he was slipping.

"Damn little bro, I didn't even think about that." Mont said looking to the ceiling.

"I got my uncle's stuffer parked in the alley. I'll drive you over there. But shit I aint got no tags or nothin'." Nacho announced.

"Boom problem solved." Mont said with a thirsty grin on

his face.

The trio briefly fumbled with a few pistols that were stashed throughout the room. The sight of them getting locked and loaded resembled a scene out of an action movie or video game before the big show down. From the boys' perspective, they felt as if they were trapped in an action movie or video game.

Cliff found it to be very taboo that his peers and even himself was so fascinated with murder. To understand that there was the possibility of himself, or someone close to him, being a killer or victim any day out the week was a very surreal feeling for the young man. Then there was the element that those who never participated could never understand, the connection between Black American youth and gangster rap. Every song felt personal because they were living it. The result turned kids like Mont, Nacho and Cliff into living testaments of the music. One could even say that they became religious in a sense and began looking to their music for answers the way their grandparents looked to their bibles.

The teens piled into the little gray stuffer that Nacho had parked in the alley. As Nacho cranked up the engine, loud music filled the small car. Mont flickered his lighter in an attempt to light the blunt he had twisted for the ride.

"A man wait until we get to the next back street to light that shit up." Nacho suggested.

"Man we ridin' dirty as fuck three niggas in a grimey lookin stuffer with no L's and I's." Mont looked over at his friend. "If the police see us we gettin stopped regardless."

Nacho half nodded as his long time friend made perfect sense. "Yea you kind of got a point there homie;"

The teens drove through North East Portland for about

10 minutes before they reached their destination. Mont took a few last minute pulls from the blunt. He checked himself out in the mirror then asked Nacho, "A man let me get some of that cheap ass cologne you always keep in here."

"Don't knock the Ocean Potion brody. Y'all know I stay pullin' all the hoes rockin' this shit. I don't know what y'all would do with out me, stay ready so you never have to get ready," Nacho taunted his friend as Cliff chuckled in the backseat. "You need some condoms too lil nigga!"

Mont held up a black box of condoms. "Nah, I still got these left over from yo' aunt Rosa's house." The whole group simultaneously erupted in laughter.

"Yea right nigga Uncle Hector will break out the feds just to whoop yo' ass." Nacho joked back.

"I'll take that ass whoopin' for my little Spanish Fly." Mont snapped back. In Black American culture it's common that good friends would roast each other. Ironically, most look at these sting sessions (or roasts) as a sign of endearrment.

Cookie sat looking out the window, watching the rain as it fell. She found this to be relaxing and was one of the many things she had missed about Portland. She had noticed a gray stuffer circle the block a few times, and then park a few houses down. At first she became upset, assuming it was JR. He had been calling and texting her non stop ever since she told him it was over the night of the party. Then she realized at once that it was probably Mont. She hurried from the window to the restroom and began brushing her teeth. She reflected on the guilty pleasure she felt after eating funions and pizza all day as she binge watched one of her favorite shows.

She quickly but gently brushed her teeth, then hair and

then applied a thin layer of lip gloss. Her phone began to ring. She clicked answer and turned it onto speaker mode so she could finish in the mirror. "Hey," She greeted Mont in her softest tone.

"I think I'm outside, which house is yours?" Mont asked.

"The brown house with the rose bushes in the yard." She answered.

"Okay, open the door pretty girl." He replied.

She hung up the phone and took one last look at herself in the mirror. She quickly removed her pizza sauce stained shirt and gray sweat pants, revealing perfectly shaped brown thighs and full round breasts. She slipped on a thinner, more fitting pair of pink sweats that she had bought from the lingerie store and a fresh white t-shirt that her breasts fought to break out of. She made her way to the front door, straightening up along the way.

Before Mont stepped out of the stuffer, he showered himself in the cologne Nacho had let him use. Then he pulled a small bottle of breath freshener out of his pocket and gave himself four or five quick sprays, to his peers' amusement. Nacho and Cliff broke out laughing.

"This nigga is definitely about to go eat the pussy!" Cliff said between chuckles.

"Right," Nacho cut in. "all these sacred eat the muff rituals this nigga doin'."

"Fuck y'all!" Mont replied, "Always hatin' on a player."

"Look Cliff, you see he aint deny it though." Nacho said as he and Cliff laughed uncontrollably.

"Fuck yall," Mont flipped his peers off as he stepped out of the car. "Just be ready to pick me up when I call y'all back,"

Mont and Nacho roared in laughter as they rode away. Mont had planned on trying to look cool when he walked up the stairs, but the comedic episode from the car made him laugh hysterically as he approached the house. When Cookie opened the door Mont was walking up the stairs cheesing ear to ear. She felt as if she would melt and returned a wide smile, revealing pearly white teeth and deep brown dimples.

"Well somebody seems to be in a good mood today!" Cookie said as she reached up to hug Mont.

"How could I not be in a good mood? I get the pleasure of yo' company today." Mont replied still cheesing.

"You so sweet," Cookie leaned her head onto Mont's chest.

Mont couldn't help but to take the opportunity to rub her perfectly shaped round booty. He thought to himself, "Yep, softer than a pillow, just like I thought."

Cookie pealed his hands off and led him towards the door. "Come in here out of that cold boy." Cookie clicked the T.V. unpaused. "Take your jacket off so I can hang it up for you." Mont handed Cookie his jacket. "Have a seat, you're welcome to turn to something different."

Mont sat down and studied the television. "What's that sweet smell comin' from the kitchen?"

"Just some hot cocoa and peanut butter cookies, you want some?" Cookie replied.

"Hell yea!." Mont quickly replied, causing Cookie to giggle. The coupled watched television and ate sweets over the next few hours, until eventually Mont and Cookie fell asleep in each other's arms.

A few miles across town, Cliff and Nacho sat in the Tillman's basement bagging up weed. "A Nacho didn't you say you knew somebody who needed some Vikes?" Cliff inquired

"Yep, what's up?" Nacho replied.

"I got like 50 of 'em right now." Cliff informed his friend.

"Well shit we could go up there once we drop this tree off." Nacho assured his friend.

Cliff's phone began to ring. He anxiously answered. "Hello,"

On the other end of the line was Taz. "What's up Nephew. It's been a change of plans. We stayin' the night out here."

"That's cool, I should be alright." Cliff replied. Taz didn't miss what his nephew said.

"Where yo' brother at? Why that little nigga aint pickin up?" Taz inquired.

"You know he don't listen to nobody. Me and Nacho dropped him off at a bitch house. Once he call back we goin' to pick him up." Mont couldn't help but to tell his uncle the truth.

"Damn that little hard headed mothafucka!" Taz roared in a deep raspy tone, "Y'all need to kick back for a minute. The last thing you want is to get caught slippin' out here movin' too much."

Yea i here you Unk," Cliff replied.

"So what y'all over there doin'?" Taz asked.

"Me and Nacho just posted waitin' on this change to come through," Cliff answered.

"Damn nigga, stay close to the crib." Taz coached his nephew.

"I know Unk. I can't let the money pass me by though. You taught me that, regardless of the situation." Cliff reasoned with his uncle.

"Man just be safe. Call me if some shit crack off." Taz was very nervous about his nephews roaming the neighborhood at a time like this.

"I got you Unk. We'll be cool, just enjoy yourself at the casino mayne. We gon' hold it down, the Killa Gang don't slip.

"Okay, be safe nephew." Taz hung up his phone and returned to his spot at the craps table. He became upset with himself as he thought again about his nephews, two boys in the field by themselves. Then he thought back to when he and his little brother were the same age, doing much worse. He downed the the tall shot of Cognac in his hand, then he threw a few chips onto the table. He could still feel the liquor burning in his throat as he spoke up, "Okay I want to play the field, all the hards and the 7's. And get the cocktail waitress for me too please."

Back in the hood, Cliff and Nacho rode the back streets of the city. Cliff counted cash as they cruised. "This shit don't stop cuddin!" Cliff exclaimed.

"Right, a nigga aint gon' stop gettin paid. On Killingsworth street homie!" Nacho replied. "What's up with Mont though? He ain't ready yet? Its almost 12:30."

"This nigga aint pickin up. He probably over there face deep." Cliff joked but neither of the young men laughed.

"Let's just go slide by there, make sure its all good." The words Nacho spoke were identical to the thought that was in Cliff's mind.

"Yep let's do it." Cliff added.

Meanwhile in Cookie's living room, she and Mont lay

cuddled up on the soft love seat that sat in front of the television. Cookie almost jumped out of her seat "Ahhhhhh!" She screamed at the top of her lungs, startling Mont.

"Damn what's wrong?" Mont asked as Cookie clinched him tighter.

"I keep having these crazy nightmares about clowns. Oh my God I'm so embarassed," Cookie wiped sweat from her brow.

"Don't be embarrassed everybody have nightmare's sometimes." Mont slowly stood up, Cookie's eyes followed his every move. "Relax I'm going to get you some cold water." Mont started toward the kitchen.

"It's some bottled water in the 'fridge." She called out from the couch. Mont returned with two ice cold bottles of water. He handed one to Cookie as he sat back down. "So you have nightmares too Lamont?" She asked in response to his earlier comment.

"Of course, its natural" Mont replied.

"So what kind of nightmares do you have?" Cookie asked innocently.

Mont thought about the nights he woke up in a cold sweat after dreaming his enemies had finally caught up with him. He quickly decided it wouldn't be a good idea to share that with his lady friend. She just wouldn't understand, he thought to himself. "I don't know I haven't had one in a long time." he replied.

"I just can't imagine you being afraid of nothin'." She spoke truthfully. Everyone around the young man could sense that he was fearless. "Do you mind if I take a few minutes to freshen up?"

Mont looked toward the time and 10 missed calls on his phone. it was 12:32 A.M. and he knew his little brother and Nacho were somewhere waiting on him to call back. "I might actually need to get goin'. Mom's went to the casino, I got to make sure little bro' cool at the house."

"I'm pretty sure your brother will be fine at home by his self." At that moment thunder shook the whole house as lightning lit the sky, causing Cookie to jump. This was followed by the sound of heavy rain pouring down. "Please Lamont, I really can't stand to be in this big scary house all by myself." She pleaded.

"Okay, I can stay with you until morning time." Mont couldn't say no to the tantalizing young brown skinned woman.

"Okay well you can go watch this in my room while I freshen up." She replied.

"Okay I'll be right up, I just need to call my little bro' real quick." Mont added.

Cookie started upstairs leaving Mont in the living room by himself. He dialed Cliff's number. After one ring Cliff answered the phone "What's up mayne?!"

"Shit where y'all at?" Mont asked.

"We sittin' outside right now." Cliff responded, but what he really meant was for his brother to come out.

Mont peaked out the window and spotted the little gray stuffer parked in front of the house. "Man it don't look like I'm gettin' out of here until at least the morning time. Uncle Taz texted me though he said they posted at the coast for the night."

"Yea he said you haven't been pickin' up the phone either." Cliff added. "Must be too busy eatin' that thang." Cliff and Nacho chuckled.

"Shut up nigga!" Mont looked over his shoulder to see if Cookie was still upstairs. "We had fell asleep watchin' T.V., we just chillin'."

"So what you want us to do? I mean we out here, but we ain't tryin' to post up all night while you eatin' that cookie nigga." Cliff couldn't help but to sting on his big brother.

"Shut up fool." Mont cut back in. "Just slide through first thing in the morning, I should be ready by like 8."

"Aight, we in the hood mayne." Cliff responded. Mont hung his phone up then headed upstairs to Cookie's bedroom.

When he entered her room he was very impressed with how organized it was. He thought twice before removing his 501's. He didn't want to be too forward or to look thirsty, but then he thought too himself she can't possibly expect for him to sleep in his pants and he damn sure didn't want to wear out the stiffness from the fresh denim. He carefully laid his belongings next to the bed. He stuffed his small pistol into his shoe then climbed into the bed.

Cookie gently dried herself off and applied lotion and body mists to her soft brown skin. She thought to herself, "Damn what am I doing?" She was a true virgin and didn't want Mont to get the wrong idea about staying the night. However, she really liked him and for some reason did not want to let him leave if she could help it. She pulled a two piece cartoon themed pajama set over her matching white lace panties and bra.

When Cookie entered the room Mont was in awe about how enchanting she truly was. Her skin was a vibrant tone of brown and the water from the shower had a curling effect on her hair. Even though she attempted to hide her body under the pajamas she wore, her curves were still very evident and Mont could smell all the sweet fragrances that she applied before entering the room.

"Damn baby, you smell like a pack of candy!" Mont complimented.

"You so crazy. Thank you." She blushed. "Hey do you have any weed? I want to relax."

"Actually I do." Mont reached over the bed and pulled a blunt out of his folded pants. Cookie turned on her internet radio and quickly the room filled with smooth music. The two teenagers laid next to each other in bed passing reefer back and forth while enjoying music.

"Do you ever wonder like why we're here? What life God meant for us to have?" Cookie asked.

"Sometimes, but then I always figure, if God is almighty and omniscient then he has the power to change anything he don't like anyway. So in a way I think we're already doin' what we were meant to do." Mont looked over to see Cookie's reaction. She was cleary fascinated with his perspective. "Like you and me, right here together sharing this moment right now. It feels so natural to be around each other because it's by devine design baby."

"You really think so," Cookie replied. She sensed a deeper side of Mont than what met the surface.

"I know so. I can feel it, can't you?" Mont said truthfully as he reached over to grab her hand. She responded to him with her soft lips on his. After about three minutes of making out, Cookie found herself laying in bed wearing only her panties as

Mont kissed, licked and sucked her lips, neck and nipples. She felt his hand crawling towards her vagina.

"Wait Mont, let's slow down." She pleaded.

"Okay, do you want me to stop?" He asked with sincerity in his tone.

"I mean I want to but I'm just not ready." Cookie spoke truthfully. "I'm sor-" She was cut off by Mont's tongue in her mouth. With out thinking he started making a trail of kisses down her body. "Mont what are you doing?" She asked. He continued down her body. From her nipples, to her stomach, than her navel, then near her panty line. He gently pinched her nipple as he kissed her thick brown thighs. She had no resistance left when he slid her panties to the side, revealing the prettiest feminine lips he had ever seen.

Mont looked up towards Cookie's face as he used his thumb to spread her tight lips apart. "I ain't never did this before Cookie, I'm really into you." She didn't have a chance to respond as he tasted her womanhood for the first time. It was one of the sweetest things to every meet his mouth. She let out a gasp as he explored her temple. Mont couldn't help but to grin as he thought to himself how his peers had teased him earlier. At this moment he didn't care though, they would never know and he was enjoying himself.

Once he felt she was ready he lifted his head and simply asked. "Can I come in?" Her body was in a state of euphora, all she could do was nod her head. She held her legs up so Mont could remove her panties. He carefully entered her virgin body as she let out another gasp. He made love to her slow and patiently. The couple spent the rest of the night exploring each others' bodies until they almost felt as if they were one. Afer reaching a climax, they laid there smoking reefer, listening to music and discussing dreams until they both fell asleep in each others' arms.

Chapter 4

When Mont woke up, he found himself still wrapped in Cookie's arms, both naked as the day they were born. He gently worked himself out of her embrace then grabbed his phone out of his pants that were folded next to the bed. He sent a text message to his little brother, "I'm up slide through."

Cookie had been awake ever since her new lover wrestled his way out of her grasp. She looked up towards Mont, "Good morning."

"Good morning pretty girl," Mont replied. "Did you sleep good?"

"Yes I did. I wish we could just lay in each other's arms all day." She spoke truthfully. She knew Mont would be leaving soon.

"Me too, but its cool we'll have time to kick it." Mont promised his new lady.

Back at the TIllmans' house, Nacho was in a kush coma on his friends' sofa. He and Cliff had been up all night smoking weed and hitting licks. Cliff entered the room. "This fool finally hit me sayin' he ready." Cliff announced groggily as he stretched.

Nacho slowly rose to his feet. He felt as if he had been out for 100 years even though it had only been about 90 minutes. "Okay well shit let's make it bro," The pair quickly got themselves together then headed out the door. After getting into the little gray stuffer, Nacho attempted to crank on the car. The first two attempts were in vain, then finally the engine roared, like a lion suffering from lung cancer. "We got to let this mothafucka heat up for a minute." Nacho declared as he adjusted the heat.

"I feel you, it's colder than a penguin's pussy out here." Cliff said between shivers.

After about 7 minutes the little gray stuffer slowly crept out the alley. The teens cruised slowly through back streets. When they reached 14th and Prescott the check engine light came on and the car began to stall.

"Fuck!" Nacho exclaimed. "This is the wrong place for this bullshit to happen. The teen's had found themselves stuck in the heart of their enemies turf. The stuffer began smoking heavily so Nacho pulled over. Just as he parked the car shut off.

"We probably just need to let it cool down and put some coolant in there." Cliff thought out loud. There was a convenience store one block away on 15th, the only problem was it was a known hang out for the Alberta Street Gang.

"Fuck it." Nacho thought out loud. The pair both cocked their pistols and made sure the safety was off. With the pistols concealed in their front hoody pockets, the teens got out of the car and started in the direction of the store.

Across the street, Randall sat on his porch watching Cliff and Nacho bail down the street. Randall wasn't officially from Alberta yet but he was definitely affiliated. He dialed his big cousin Tic. A deep husky voice answered "What's up little cuddin?"

"A couple of them niggas bailin' through the hood right now cuddy." Randall axniously told his big cousin.

"Where you at?" Tic asked.

"I'm at the house, they just walked in the store. I don't think either of these ones did it, but they was definatley with the nigga who popped Junee." Randall had no idea that Cliff was the actual shooter.

*Yep I'm about to pull up on 'em Murda Gang." Tic responded.

As soon as Nacho came out the store he noticed the white sedan cruising in thier direction down Prescott. At first he couldn't remember where he had saw the car at before, then it came to him. It was the same car Junee and Tic were in after the party, he was sure of it. "Watch out Cliff," Nacho held his arm out stopping his friend in his tracks. "That's them bitch ass niggas right there."

Cliff felt his stomach tighten. "What you tryin' to do?"

"Whatever its gon' take to get us up out of here." It was understood between the two long time friends what time it was.

They continued walking back toward their vehicle as Tic's car approached. The teens tried to play it cool at first but once Cliff and Tic made eye contact, the quiet street quckly turned into a battlefield. Cliff and Nacho started busting shots in the car's direction, leaving several bullet holes in the door.

Tic let off about three shots before franticly pulling over behind an SUV that was parked. He hopped out with the engine still running. He carefully crept in the teens' direction ducking behind cars along the way.

"Damn that nigga still movin!" Nacho exclaimed. "I'm almost out of slugs."

"Me too," Cliff added just as Tic emerged from behind a car letting off shots in the teens' direction. Two of the lightning fast bullets caught Nacho in the stomach and shin. His injured limb gave out as he collapsed to the ground mid step. With his last bullet he missed horribly hitting a parked car.

"Fuck!" Nacho exclaimed as he laid bleeding on the cold cement.

Tic turned his attention towards Cliff. There was only two shots left in Cliff's snub-nosed .380 while Tic's .45 had an extended clip protruding from it's handle. BANG! BANG! Cliff's last two shots were unrewarding. Now Tic stood face to face with his young rival. There was an evil sneer across Tic's face, it appeared as if he was possessed by a demon. When he realized Cliff was out of ammo his sneer turned to an evil grin as he held his bulky pistol only inches away from the teen's face.

Cliff's face was full of terror and remorse. He saw flashes of his childhood clear as day. He couldn't believe it but had to accept his current circumstance. He could feel the grim reaper's cold breath on the back of his neck as he got goose bumps all over.

Tic squeezed as hard as he could on the trigger of his pistol, to his disappointment. He squeezed a few more times and nothing. Cliff was just as surprised as Tic when the large pistol didn't bark.

"FUCK!" Tic cursed the pistol for jamming. He turned on his heels and darted back toward his bullet ridden vehicle.

As the the white sedan sped away Cliff came to his friend's aid. "Come on bro, we got to get out of here." Sirens could be heard approaching the scene. Nacho still laid helpless on the ground.

"I ain't goin nowhere no time soon. Just take my thang and get out of here. I'll be cool." Nacho assured his friend.

"Naw fuck that, I can't leave you here." Cliff's loyalty was times a million for his homies. He felt if he left and Nacho died it would some how be his fault.

"I only got hit in the leg. Ain't no sense in the police knowin' that we was both here and both of us goin' to jail. Trust me I'll be cool. Get up out of here little North East Sider, we solid." Nacho didn't realize he also had a slug in his abdomen, he thought he hurt all over from falling to pavement. He knew that somehow the police would find a way to arrest Cliff if he was at the scene when they arrived. Cliff nodded and darted back toward Killingsworth.

By the time the police and paramedics had arrived to the scene, Cliff had made it back to his own turf. He power walked through the alley that led to the back door of his home. He had been walking so fast and breathing so hard that he didn't hear his phone ringing almost the whole way. After entering his house he discovered the 7 missed calls from Mont. He attempted to call Mont back, only to be greeted by Mont's obnoxious voice mail.

"FUCK!" He said out loud. He thought to himself maybe his brother was still waiting at Cookie's house. He tried to relax as he lit a half smoked blunt that was in his ashtray.

Meanwhile, Mont accepted Cookie's offer for a ride home. He attempted to play it cool but seemed very agitated and uneasy when his little brother and Nacho didn't answer the phone.

"Damn If Mom comes home and we not there that's gon' be my ass!" The statement was only for Cookie's benefit. He didn't want to scare the innocent girl away. Although she had already heard about Mont and his friends from her cousins, she just nodded and accepted his explanation about his anxiousness.

When the couple drove past 12th & Prescott they both noticed the police tape and ambulance a couple blocks away. They were too far for Mont to realize that it was Nacho on the stretcher in back of the ambulance. He silently prayed that his brother and friend were safe. Cookie noticed his change in demeanor.

"Everything okay Lamont?" She asked in her most sincere tone of voice.

"I'm straight baby," He replied still looking out the window.

Cookie broke the long silence when they finally pulled in front of Mont's house. "You alright baby? Want me to stay for a little bit?" Cookie knew what Mont was thinking, but didn't want to directly ackowledge what he feared.

"Naw, its cool baby," Mont replied calmly. "I'll call you once I get my phone charged up." He reached his face in for a kiss. Her lips met his for a brief exchange.

"Okay, I'll see you later." She said as she watched Mont climb out of the car. At this point Cookie wasn't sure what she'd gotten herself into by becoming involved with Mont. She felt his passion and fury when they made love. She could sense that something serious was happening but was still too naive to fully understand the situation. Over the past couple days it seemed as if the more acquainted she became with Mont, the pretty city she grew up in became an eerie dangerous place she was not familiar with.

Shortly after Cookie pulled off, Taz and Retha pulled up to the house. Taz left the engine running as he walked into to the house straight to the basement. Cliff was suprised to see his brother and uncle walk down the stairs about ten paces apart. At first he assumed that they had already knew what had happened to Nacho. After giving them the rundown Cliff's big brother and uncle both felt like they were at fault for what happened. Eventually, while alone Taz shed a tear picturing his nephew with a gun in his face.

Later, at Emanuel Hospital, Nacho felt like two giants had played tennis using him as the ball. The majority of his time there, gang task consistently came into the room interrogating him about what happened and other recent crimes that were happening in the area. Nacho knew he was on the radar when he got a visit from Detective Walker.

Walker was known for taking down gang bangers since the '90s. He was the main detective on Latrezz' case and it seemed like since he was acquitted Walker's agression toward young black men was focused specifically on the Killlingsworh gang. Nacho called Mont from his Mother's phone since his had been confiscated.

"What's up brody," Nacho asked in a low tone.

"What's up Killa Gang, the homies was tryin' to get up there but Stomp said they wouldn't let nobody see you." Mont responded.

"Don't trip homie. Gang task been standin' outside my door. Walker tryin' to get some information he keep askin' what happened comin' in here at 2 in the mornin' when Im high off oxy's and shit." Nacho took a deep swig of the cold apple juice on his lunch tray. "Today this peckawood dropped a warrant on my lap and asked me did I want to talk now."

"What you tell him?" Mont asked.

"I told him to do what he need to do. This shit say they found my prints on a shell case but I think it's some bullshit.

Tell the homies to kick back they probably takin' me straight downtown after I get checked out. I don't want nobody caught up," Nacho advised his friend. Mont trusted Nacho would never snitch and understood exactly what his homie was trying to communicate to him. "A though, I need somebody to get my lunch out the stuffer over there once it's cool. Get the keys from my Mom."

"Don't trip Killa Gang, I got you homie." Mont was excited at the thought of going back to his rivals turf.

After only four days in the hospital, Nacho was checked out and arrested by Walker. He was booked into jail still wearing a cast and bandages. He spent the first seven hours of his incarceration being beaten and interrogated by Walker and his goons. True to his form, Nacho kept it gangster and didn't give up any information on who shot him, how his fingerprints ended up on shell casings or who he was with. He was officially charged with attempted murder and unlawful use of weapon even though he was the only vicitim and no weapon was found. Walker knew it was a weak case, but his main objective was to apply pressure to the Killingsworth Gang.

Mont grinned to himself as he reminisced on what happened when he went to retrieve Nacho's belongings from the broke down stuffer, still parked on 14th. He and Cliff sat in the back seat as they pointed out the stuffer to Taz and Black. "We parked it right there." Cliff pointed as they slowly rolled down the street. Black parked his '90's Cadillac behind the stuffer. Mont reached for the door handle.

"What you doin'? You too hot let me grab that shit." Taz spoke up.

"I know where all his stash spots is though." Mont reasoned with his uncle.

"I'll hop out with him Taz," Black spoke up, "Get behind the wheel. if somebody try somethin' I'm blastin'." Taz nodded as his nephew and homie hopped out and went through the abandoned stuffer. Taz and Cliff stayed in the car fondling their pistols, constantly checking the rear view mirror and windows. After about a minute Mont and Black re-entered the Cadillac.

"Damn my nigga Nacho hot!" Mont announced. "This nigga had like two zones of nascar in there!" Just as the group was pulling off a group of young men walked out of the store.

"Y'all recognize them niggas?" Black asked.

"I know for sure the one with the beenie on is a brand." Mont informed the rest of the group. That confirmation was all it took to set Taz and Black into action. Without discussion Taz pulled back over, once parked he and Black quickly exited the car with their pistols in hand. Mont and Cliff were both infatuated at the sight of the two men in the middle of the street dumping on the opposition.

As the group scattered Taz and Black climbed back into the Cadillac. "Hit the corner I want to get off on 'em too!" Mont blurted out excitedly. Taz quickly turned the corner after the young men as Mont and Black let off shots from the passenger side windows of the car. "KILLA GANG!!!" Mont yelled out, his words muffled by the sound of gunfire. Later the news would report that two men in their 20's suffering injuries from gunshots checked into Emanuel. Since that incident they had not seen a single Alberta Gangster on the street, or a Killingsworth Gangster either.

It was the last week of winter break before the teens went back to school. Taz and Mont had been on the hunt every night since Nacho got popped. They took to the streets shooting at anyone who they recognized to be a member of the Alberta Gang. After a few nights of this, word spread of the various shootings around the city and the streets became a ghost town. It was the last Friday before school was back in, the pair had grown bored of riding through North and North East Portland the past two days with no enemies in sight.

Two days had passed since they had any action, however Mont insisted his uncle picked him up just like the nights prior to this one. "Let's hit the liquor store Unk." Mont suggested as he looked calmly out the window. Taz just nodded and turned his vehicle in the direction of the liquor store. As soon as they turned on M.L.K. Boulevard Mont spotted Tic across the street. "Oooh! Oooh!." He almost jumped out of the moving vehicle.

Taz became excited with his nephew. "Who is that nigga?" Taz honestly had no idea what Tic or Junee looked like. Around the time of their incarceration they had just became active.

"That's that nigga Tic right there Unk! Pull up I'm about to get this nigga." Mont started to roll down his window.

"Hold up nephew, we got to get up close and personal to make sure we do it right," Taz stated calmly as he pulled to the side street behind the liquor store. "Look he about to go in the store, as soon as he come out I'm gon' light his ass up."

"Let me get him Unk, these niggas think I'm playin' about my little brother." Mont was thirsty for a body and his uncle felt the same way. The difference was that Taz was no stranger to murder while Mont had shot plenty but killed none, yet.

"We talkin' about life in the bing nephew," Taz looked his nephew square in the eye. "You ready for that?"

Mont pulled his hood over his head. "It's already done Unk, this Killa Gang!"

Tic spent about five minutes in the store. After paying for his drink he headed towards the door. When he stepped outside he felt a stillness in the air. It seemed as if the city was sleep. There were no people out and no cars on the road. He looked over his shoulder only to discover an empty street. Tic looked up to the sky and saw the moon peaking at him through the clouds. As he turned to walk away he took a deep breath of the crisp fresh air that surrounded him.

BANG! BANG! BANG! BANG! BANG! All he seen was the gun's muzzle before his massive body collapsed to the pavement. He lay there with his eyes wide open and blood oozing from his mouth. The last thing he would ever see was the fading blurry image of black Chuck Taylor's running away into the darkness.

Chapter 5

Latrezz slept like a bear in the winter, until his slumber was interupted by the obnoxious beeping from his alarm clock. Latrezz opened his eyes then leaned over and pressed the snooze button. Once the beeping stopped, the room was filled briefly with static followed by soul music. The time on the clock read 5:03.

He stretched as he stood up and stepped into his slippers, then walked sleepishly out of the room. He entered the bathroom with his eye's closed. Latrezz spent about seven minutes brushing his teeth and washing his face the way Mrs. Tillman did when he was a boy. Once he was finished grooming himself, he reached behind the mirror and grabbed a blunt out of the cabinet.

It was barely dawn, as Latrezz opened the sliding screen door into his back yard. His pit bull puppy came darting from behind him, anxious to relieve herself. He named her Brandy because she was dark brown. Latrezz paced slowly around his back yard taking drags from his blunt. At times he would stop to medal his puppy.

"G-Get yo' ass from there Brandy!" He ordered between coughs. She quickly moved from the spot near the fence where she had been digging and ran up to Latrezz wagging her tail. He pet her on the head and walked back into his house with his puppy in toe.

Within fifteen minutes, Latrezz had finished taking a shower and brushing his teeth again. He picked a pair of 501's and a white thermal out of his closet. After sliding on a pair of shoes and his bomber jacket he was ready to go.

Just as he started toward the door he stopped in his tracks and went to the drawer next to his bed. He fumbled through the clothes revealing a hand gun, then continued searching until he uncovered a text book. "Okay now I'm ready," He thought to himself as he placed the book in his bag and headed outside.

When Latrezz pulled up to the corner store he saw his nephews. They stood near the front entrance paying close attention to the passing cars. No one noticed the faint blood splatter on Mont's shoes.

"What's up nephews?" Latrezz greeted the teens as he stepped out of his car.

"What's up uncle 'Trezz." Cliff Responded.

"Wasup Unk. Where you headed to?" Mont asked. He wasn't sure if his uncle was aware of his new status yet.

"I'm headed to this class my brotha." Latrezz responded in a sarcastic tone. "Since yall out here this early I take it that y'all headed to school too."

Mont tried to sound like his uncle's when he spoke, but his voice wasn't deep enough yet. "I might stop through there around lunch time to get off some of this bud."

"Naw you'll be there at 8 homie." Latrezz assured his nephew in a stern voice. "And what the hell was you doin last night? Yo' Mama was blowin' me up lookin for you fool!"

Mont responded calmly, "I don't know why she was trippin'. Uncle Taz came to pick me up."

"Oh what did y'all end up getting into?" Latrezz knew that Nacho had been shot but was unaware of his nephews connection to the incident.

"Not shit really. Served one of them niggas in front of the liquor store, smoking and shit. Nothing too exciting." Mont looked up toward Latrezz to see what his response would be.

Cliff stood with his hands in his pockets, avoiding eye contact with his uncle.

Latrezz looked toward Mont and Cliff then took a deep breath. "Be careful out here mayne."

"You know I got that." Mont said grinning as he patted his pocket.

"Whats up with my little nigga Nacho?" Latrezz asked.

"They found his prints on some shells on the scene and booked him for an attempt. They tryin' to hit him with Measure 11." Mont briefed his uncle.

"Who else got shot?" Latrezz didn't notice Cliff's demeanor change.

Cliff spoke up. "Nobody, them peckawoods wanted a case cuddin wouldn't give 'em one so they put one one him." Cliff looked away. "He solid though, he could've threw me under the bus but didn't mention me."

Latrezz shook his head as he entered the convenient store and walked straight to the back. He stopped at the refrigerator, and grabbed a bottle of water. He laid his drink and a five dollar bill on the counter.

"Let me get a pack of cigars too." There was no need to say which cigar. Latrezz had been shopping at the same corner store since he was a kid so the petite Asain lady behind the counter already knew what he wanted. She handed him a pack of Chocolate Phillies and put the cash in the register with out speaking a word.

Latrezz exited the store and approached his nephews again. "Let ya unk get some of that medicine neph'."

"What you need." Mont asked grinning ear to ear.

Latrezz returned his nephews boyish grin, "A dime for the set price."

Mont reached in his hoody pocket then made the exchange during what appeared to be a handshake. "Let me know when you ready for me to put you on the hood." Mont said with a smirk on his face.

"The only problem with that is you cant whoop my ass... B.G." Latrezz playfully shoved Mont as he approached his car. He partially opened the door then looked toward the teens. "Make sure you make it to school today."

"I got you unk." Mont replied

Latrezz got back in his car and drove away. After talking to his nephews he felt torn. On one hand he felt he was doing the right thing by setting a good example for them, on the other hand he felt like they needed his guidance in the streets and felt bad about not riding with them.

Latrezz pressed the button on his blue tooth ear piece. "What's up bro?"

On the other end of the line Taz sat at the table in his kitchen smoking a cigarette. "Shit, thinkin' about takin a little retreat."

"Damn Taz," Latrezz knew his brother well enough to know why he needed to skip town.

"It aint shit little bro. I'm just gon' take nephew to see some family and we gon' be back two weeks tops." Taz assured his little brother.

"Damn why you got him rollin' with you anyway." Latrezz asked as he cruised through traffic.

"Miss me with that square shit right now homie. You know how it is out here shit happens. You probably talkin' to me on that damn Bluetooth right now." Taz knew his little brother was right but also was still religous about thugging the same way Latrezz used to be.

Latrezz' facial expressioned turned into an irritated scowl as the light on his earpiece blinked. "What ever man. I'll be over there."

"Cool," Taz replied then hung the phone up. Although they had not been on the same page since Latrezz beat his case, the brothers were still best friends and had a mutual understanding that only brothers could share.

Later, in the back hallways of Jefferson High School, Mont & Cliff shot dice with four other teenagers including Randall. One of the teens shook the dice and tossed them against the wall.

"There go the nina ross right there. Ugh." The teen snapped as the dice hit the ground.

Cliff looked puzzled. "What? Nina ross? Thats burnt money fool!"

The teen with the dice looked up toward Cliff. "What?!"

"Your point was eight homie." Mont declared in a stern voice.

"I said it was nine so its nine." The teen on the dice replied.

"You can say what you want but I needs mines homie." Cliff said as he balled his fists.

"Fuck you!" The other teen said as he reached for the pile of money. Cliff reached over and punched him in the face. The pair engaged in a violent scuffle. Mont pulled a set of brass knuckles out of his pocket as the other teens approached him.

"What you heard about Big Tic getting popped last night?" Randall asked.

Mont's facial expression was one of disbelief as if he seen a ghost. "What? I aint heard shit, what's up?"

Randall continued to interrogate Mont, "Well that's my big cousin and..." SMACK!!! Mont struck Randall in the face with the brass knuckles causing him to crumble. He quickly struck another teenager with a similar blow. The last teen in the group viciously punched Mont on the back of the head knocking him to the ground.

The teens barbarously stomped Mont until a feminine voice called out, "What in the hell is goin' on in here with all this damn ruckus?"

Randall, and the other teens pulled their friend from Cliff's grasp throwing cheap shots at him the whole time. As the four teenagers ran down the hallway, Cliff and Mont used the wall and each other for balance as they stumbled to their feet. Cliff's shirt was ripped and Mont's face was badly bruised.

When Ms. Jones came around the corner her hands flew to her mouth at the sight of the injured Tillman brothers. "Oh my GOD! What happened? Are you boys okay? Who did this?" Mont and Cliff didn't say anything to the concerned lady as she escorted them to the school nurse.

Meanwhile, on the SouthWest side of town Mont sat at his desk in the back the classroom. He'd enrolled at Portland State University the previous fall. Latrezz enjoyed expanding his mind and gaining knowledge. However the primary reason he went everyday was to stay out of trouble and set a better example for his nephews.

In the front of the room a black man in his fifties flipped through the pages of a text book on his desk. Professor Thomas had been an instructor for almost twenty years. He still wore his hair in a salt & pepper colored Afro and his wardrobe was comparable to Cliff Huxstable. Even though he dressed very neat, Latrezz was always baffled at how ashy Professor Thomas' knuckles appeared. In the seat next to Latrezz sat Katie, she was a white woman in her twenties with dreadlocks and several visible piercings and tattoos. Latrezz knew had he not been in this class he would've never befriended the caucasian hippy.

Katie leaned toward Latrezz. "Hey Latrezz," she whipsered.

"What's up," He replied very softly.

Katie's dimple peircings rose on her face as she grinned. "You got a dub?"

"Yea, I thought you sold bud." He replied.

She giggled holding a hand over her mouth. "I do but I like that shit from your side of town."

Latrezz joined Katie in laughter, "Fasho holla at me after class."

"Mr. Tillman?" Professor Thomas called out from the front of the room.

Latrezz very calmly responded, "Professor Thomas,"

"Can you answer the question?" The elder of the two men asked.

"Can you repeat the question?" Latrezz confidently responded.

"According to the text what are three common causes for mental instability?" Professor Thomas asked as he removed his glasses from his face and folded his arms.

Latrezz was leaned back in his seat like it was a pimp mobile. He replied with, "High anxiety, depression or chronic drug use." He winked at Katie after using the word "chronic" causing her to giggle.

Professor Thomas' eyes grew large, he was astonished by the easy going student's response. "Correct. However, that still does not grant you the privilege of speaking while I'm speaking. Please save your fraternizing for after class."

"I got you." Latrezz responded nonchalauntly.

Once the class was over several students poored into the hallway. Latrezz and Katie headed toward the door. Professor Thomas sat at his desk thumbing through a thick text book. "Mr. Tillman, may I have a word with you?"

Latrezz and Katie both stopped and turned around. "I'll be in the parking lot." Katie announced as she patted her friends shoulder and continued out of the classroom.

Latrezz approached Professor Thomas' desk. "What's up?"

"You're one of my best students. Why is it you always have a lot to say but only participate in the class discussion when put on the spot?" Professor Thomas grilled him. He saw alot of potential in Latrezz but couldn't understand why he wasn't a model student.

Latrezz shrugged his shoulders. "I don't know?"

"Well I'd appreciate it if you started participating a little more. I read your paper and you had some really good points." He spoke truthfully. "I'm very impressed by your intellect and perspective Mr. Tillman."

"Thank you," The compliment caught Latrezz off guard. He had never been praised for anything before, well except being a gangster.

Professor Thomas pat Latrezz on the back. "Alright, come prepared to speak next class."

"Okay." Latrezz nodded then walked out of the room.

Back in the hood, Retha sat impatiently holding her phone to her ear. When she was angry her eyes lit up the same as her brothers'. Although she was in her mid 30s, the only thing that gave away her age was her boys. Her brown skin was still vibrant and she knew how to dress. The more time that passed, the more her sons started to remind her of her brothers. She could recall Taz and Latrezz spending their teenage years always in some kind of drama. Now here she was, experiencing parenthood as her mother did years ago.

FInally, the phone stopped ringing. "Where you at Nut?" she snapped in a fiesty tone.

Latrezz sat in the front seat of Katie's smoke filled car holding his phone to his ear in one hand and a blunt in another. He attempted to take drags between speaking. "Damn, and hello to you too." Latrezz responded coughing.

Her little brother's sarcastic response only agitated her more. "I don't have time for no jokes right now. I just got off the phone with Ms. Jones, your nephews got into a fight at school today."

Latrezz sat up with the phone to his ear as he passed the blunt to Katie. "With each other?" He asked sounding confused.

"No, she said they wouldn't tell her nothin' but from the looks of things it was more of the other ones than them. She say some of the other students been sayin' its some gang bull shit goin' on." Retha informed her little brother.

"So what do you want me to do?" Latrezz asked.

"To go pick 'em up and give 'em a talk on the way home. Try to see what the hell is goin on." She felt Latrezz would let her know what the situation was if he knew. She also felt as if he was partly responsible for their behavior.

"Okay, We'll be over there." He responded.

"Oh, you must have misunderstood me." She replied brusquely, "They're not comin' over my house with that gang bull shit. They can stay with you since they want to follow yall's foot steps!"

Latrezz' facial expression was full of surprise. "I don't know what you talkin' about? I'm a college student."

Retha sat scratching a lottery ticket with a quarter. "And that's why I called you instead of Taz." Then she hung up the phone.

Latrezz placed his phone back in his pocket. "I got to cut. I'll catch you later."

Katie was slumped in the driver seat. She sat up and stretched, "Alrighty then."

When he pulled up to the highschool, he reflected on his time there. He could remember spending his days gambling, hustling and catching fades. He also reminisced about all of his friends that had passed away or who were serving time. A cold chill ran down his spine. Latrezz looked over his shoulder then continued up the stairs to the front entrance of the shcool.

Latrezz entered the main office and approached the desk. The receptionist was a black woman in her fifties with gray hair and thick glasses. "How may I help you sir?" She asked.

"I'm here to pick up my nephews, Clifford and Lamont Tillman." He replied in a polite voice.

"Okay, have a seat and they'll be right out." She

assured him.

Detective Walker entered the room wearing a tacky suit jacket holding a large yellow envelope. Walker took a double glance at Latrezz then approached him. "Well, well, well… If it aint my old buddy Latrezz."

Latrezz looked up twisting his face. "What's up you still hangin' around here harassin the kids man?" The hatred between the two men was mutual.

"If by that you mean making life a living hell for wise guys like you, then yea. Are you still hurting people for your set homie?" Walker snapped back.

"I don't know what you're talkin' about. I'm a college student and I go to work full time. I don't partake in illegal activity." Latrezz said, sounding annoyed. Even though deep down he knew that he was blessed to have dodged prison.

"Well how about I search you? You smell like a pound." Walker was serious as he took a step closer to Latrezz.

"Look man I'm just up here to pick up my nephews." Cliff and Mont entered the room bruised and scarred, followed by Ms. Jones.

"Im investigating a homicide. I believe that the incident that happened today was connected. Now I see you up here. If I find out you have something to do with this I will put you away. For good this time… NUT!!!" Walker's face turned red as a tomato.

"And if you kiss your wife in the mouth tonight you'll know how my kids taste." Latrezz replied with a sinister grin on his face. Walker twisted his face as Mont and Cliff snickered.

Latrezz and his nephews cruised through traffic smoking reefer. Latrezz turned the music down. "Y'all's Mama said that yall comin' to stay with me for a second. But what was that shit about?"

"I'm guessin that was his cousin last night. I need to holla at Uncle Taz." Mont spoke up.

"That's where we're headed." Latrezz responded. The teens brought their uncle up to speed on the events that had taken place over the past couple weeks. It was now clear to him that his nephew was a klller. He was dissappointed but not surprised, Latrezz knew first hand how it easy it could be to cross that line.

Latrezz' car pulled up in front of Taz house. Latrezz exited the vehicle and walked around to the basement entrance in the back with his nephews in tow. When they entered the room Taz sat at a table counting money. Taz looked up but never stopped what he was doing. "What happened to yall?"

"Got into it." Cliff responded casusally.

Mont anxiously spoke up. "It aint shit though I'll go through there tonight for me and my little brother!"

"Naw you not. You gon sit yo' ass down for a second." Latrezz responded in a stern voice.

"Uncle Taz," Mont whined.

Taz held his hand up. "Don't put me in the middle of it. That's your uncle too and he a G from the hood you have to respect him. So just sit your little ass down at Nut house and first thing in the morning we gotta jet."

"Who was that fool?" Latrezz asked.

"Rick or Tic or somethin' I don't know." Taz responded still counting his money.

"Got faded like the rest of 'em." Mont added trying to sound hard for his uncles.

Taz observed the angry facial expression his little brother made. "He sound like you before you turned into a square."

"Shut up fool!" Latrezz responded.

Taz let out a deep husky chuckle. "Take them home I got to go make some runs with the homies."

"Aight," Latrezz felt that no matter how hard he distanced himself from the street, he could never distance himself from his family. He thought to himself maybe that justs how it was meant to be, it was where he belonged in the universe. His wretched destiny.

Chapter 6

Latrezz ironed his work shirt as his nephews ate at the dining room table. He enjoyed the idea of having the boys around and felt that it would help him prepare for his own baby.

"Aight I'm about to go to work. I wont be back until three but its plenty food in there and y'all don't need to go no where either. Its too dangerous right now." The boys just nodded as Latrezz walked out.

Mont and Cliff sat around watching television for over an hour. After growing bored of this, Mont stood up and walked to the coat rack near the door. He pulled his black hoody on. "A I'm about to go see what I see real quick. Hold down the spot little bro."

"You heard what Uncle 'Trezz said, it's hot out there right now." Cliff wished his big brother would just listen sometimes but knew he couldn't tell his hard headed sibling anything.

"That's why you're stayin' here. By the time he get home I'll be back." Mont said as he slipped on his gloves.

Cliff looked toward Mont then let out a sigh. "Aight man."

"Where yo' thang at?" Mont asked as he pulled his beenie on.

"Look in the closet." Cliff pointed toward the closet near the door.

Mont walked over to the closet and retreived the pistol. What Cliff didn't know was Mont had promised Cookie he woulld come over. Mont kept this to himself because he knew in his mind that his hormones got Nacho shot. However, he just couldn't resist the shapely brown skinned girl, who had given him her virginity days before.

Across town Big Sherm sat in his lavishly furnished basement eating chicken at his table. His fat black fingers were shiny from all of the grease. His woman, Toya, sat next to him playing solitary. While he was obese and sometimes grimy looking, she was petite and cute. On the other end of the table Black sat rolling blunts.

After hearing someone knocking at the door, Big Sherm licked his fingers and took a break from his food. "Can you get that for me baby?"

Toya stood up and approached the door as Big Sherm continued to eat. Once Toya opened the door, Taz walked into the garage. She pulled the door shut behind him as they walked toward the table.

"What's up Toya." Taz asked casually.

"Hey Taz." She responded.

"What's up Taz." Black asked as he reached for a handshake.

"What's up Black, Big Sherm." Taz shook hands with the men at the table then sat down.

"What's up homie. Toya, fix Taz a plate." Big Sherm ordered.

"Its all gone." She replied softly.

Big Sherm pulled a large roll of bills out of his pocket. He peeled a bill from the roll and held it out toward Toya. "Go by Jack's and get a twenty piece." It wasn't that he was concerned about his friend eating, it was just apart of the G-Code not to discuss business around women.

"Okay Daddy," Toya took the bill and walked out the door.

Sherm wiped his hands off with a handkerchief and then began picking his teeth with a toothpick. Once Black locked the door Big Sherm spoke up. "What do you need me to get rid of?"

Taz' gloved hand pulled a small pistol out of his pocket and placed it on the table. "Some baby shit," Black stepped closer to the table. "That mothafucka got a body on it from the other night, don't get no prints on it."

Black cheesed ear to ear, he recognized Mont's weapon. "Y'all got them boys just as bad as y'all was!"

Sherm's eyes grew large as he examined the small pistol. "That's clean too. Black put that in the stash spot for me." Black wrapped a bandana around the gun before removing it from the table then exited the room. Big Sherm stood up and walked to a safe in the corner of the room. It seemed like with every step he took another chicken crumb rolled down his shirt then fell off of his fat belly. He opened the safe and pulled out a black duffle bag then placed it on the table in front of Taz.

Taz started looking through the bag. "Just take the whole bag I got plenty more and you're goin' to need it." Big Sherm spoke the truth. Although it had been over a year since the two gangs took a loss to one another, when ever the three decade old fued was sparked the whole city became deadly.

Meanwhile in the Irving District, Mont and Cookie sat on her bed smoking weed and listening to music. She rubbed his back tenderly then asked. "What's goin' on Lamont? I feel like you ain't never got time for me no more."

"Ain't nothin' goin' on." He took a deep breath. "I be meaning to call you but I just be gettin' caught up tryin' to get this money."

She knew he was lying but didn't want to upset him by prying deeper. "Well if you ever need anything don't be afraid to ask. It could just be between us, I don't mind helping you out."

Had it been any other girl in the neighborhood, Mont would have taken his opportunity to access her pockets. However, he genuinely liked her and didn't want to burn that bridge. The only time he felt like himself was when he was alone with her.

"Naw, it aint like that baby girl." He wrapped his arm around her waist. "All I need from you is you."

She leaned over and kissed him in the mouth. Soon they were both nude, tangled in each other. Mont attempted to pull away from the amorous love making. "Damn baby, I really got to go." He forced the words out as he was partially hypnotized from her big perky cocoa colored titties, which appeared to be staring at him.

She looked him in the eyes and bit her bottom lip as she thrusted her hips toward his. "No, just stay a little longer. I don't know how long I'm going to have to go with out seeing you again."

Mont thought to himself about the noxious events that he'd recently engaged in. Any given day he could find himself incarcerated or on the wrong end of a bullet. With this in mind he figured he might as well enjoy himself in the present moment. He leaned down and kissed her in the mouth, then guided her body so that he was behind her. He smacked her on the ass causing her to arch her back, making her picture perfect booty appear even larger.

She looked back towards him, "Be gentle baby, I'm still recovering from last tim-," She let out a deep gasp as he pushed inside of her. Mont didn't blink once as her ass bounced against his thighs and belly over and and over again. Without even realizing he was at his limit, he grew weak all over. Cookie let out a deep moan as she felt her womb being filled with Mont's warm cemen. He collapsed next to her.

"Damn Lamont, you wasn't wearin' no condom?!" She asked as she felt the warm slimy liquid running down her thighs.

"At what point, did I have an opportunity to put a condom on?" Mont asked, never opening his eyes or raising from his sleep like position. She thought back to how he almost left but she pulled him back. Cookie hopped up and rushed to the shower.

After about five minutes Cookie's phone began to ring. Mont reached for the phone without opening his eyes, assuming it was his, "Hello," he said groggily.

"Nigga who the fuck is this?!" JR asked from the other end of the line.

Mont finally opened his eyes and looked at the phone. Once he realized who he was speaking with he became alive again. "You know who it is bitch ass nigga! What that Killingsworth like fool!"

"Oh okay, yea I got somethin' for you, watch out nigga!" JR fired back.

"Whatever nigga," Mont hung up the phone just as Cookie came back into the room wrapped in a towel. "You still fuckin' with JR?" he asked sharply.

"No baby, what made you ask that?" She responded in a pleading tone.

"This nigga just called you." He replied curtly.

"I promise I told him we were through. I can't help that he called me Lamont." She responded honestly. "You not mad at me are you?"

Mont believed her, but still he had business to attend to in the streets. His breif conversaion with JR only fueled his anger. "It's cool baby. I got to go though, I'll call you later." They kissed and held each other for what seemed like an eternity. Then Mont headed out the door, not realizing that he had just created life.

Mont peddled his bike down the street. After riding through his rival's turf for about five minutes, he found what he was looking for. He parked and approached a group of black teenagers on the corner. Randall was amongst the group of young men.

"What's up with that shit you was hollerin' at school." Mont called out as he appraoched the group.

"What's up?" Randall replied as he and the other teenagers approached Mont with their fists balled up. Mont reached into his pocket and pulled out the snub nosed .380 he borrowed from his brother. Just as the other teens turned around to run, Mont opened fire. BANG! BANG! BANG! BANG! One of the boys, Rodney, collapsed as he attempted to flee. Mont turned around and ran back to his bike then let off a couple more shots before speeding away into the night.

As Mont sped through the dark back streets of North East Portland he couldn't help but to laugh to himself. He felt that his rivals weren't ready to war with his caliber of gangster. With all of the shootings going on in the city they should've known better than to be hanging out, with out a pistol.

Meanwhile, word was spreading between the Alberta Gang that it was on sight with Mont. JR had even camped out down the street from Cookie's house hoping that Mont would show. However, it was too late, he was long gone back to his own turf. JR decided to go meet up with his big homies at the bar. Even though he was only 17, he could still get in because his uncle worked the door and he sold dope to the owner.

The Swan Island warehouse Latrezz worked at was filled with machinery, forklifts and boxes. There was constant heavy foot traffic. Some of the employees wore goggles, hard hats and gloves. Latrezz wore his headphones to drown out the constant buzzing mixed with beeps and other machinery sounds. Finally there was a very loud buzz, followed by the relieving sounds of all the different machines shutting down. All of the employees began to disperse from their posts and work areas. Latrezz dropped his final palette, then climbed off of the forklift he drove. He walked to a vending machine to purchase a soda.

The supervisor, Donald, was a white man in his 40s who sported grease stained Dickie shirts and thick glasses. He approached Latrezz. "Good work out there today Latrezz." Donald complimented as he pulled his gloves off.

"Thanks," Latrezz replied.

"How do you feel about becoming full time?" Donald asked.

Latrezz couldn't hold back his smile, this was the news he had wished for ever since he got hired two months prior. "That sounds pretty good to me. I have to see how it works with my school schedule though."

"Okay, well stop by my office and we can go over schedules." He started to walk away, then turned back. "By the way, there's a two dollar raise in it for you too."

Latrezz felt good as he walked through the parking lot to his car. He waved at an older white man as he stepped in his car. As he drove through the rain soaked streets of Swan Island, he laughed to himself. He reflected back on his teen years when he would come to the docks to rip off ship cargo.

After making a quick stop at a drive through restaurant, Latrezz was on his way again. He dialed his woman's number. "What you doin?" He asked casually.

On the other end of the line, Sandy lie in her bed rubbing her protruding pregant belly. Even though she was pregnant her smooth features were still soothing to look at. She had a golden brown complextion and her hair hung just past her shoulders. "Layin' down what's up?"

"Just got off of work. I was goin' to roll through there if you was goin' to be up." He responded.

"I'm not feelin' good. I might be sleep by the time you get here." Sandy wished that Latrezz would just move in with her. She stayed away from the subject though because it always sparked an argument. She wasn't aware that some nights Latrezz would wake up in a cold sweat. He was haunted by dimented nightmares about his enemies and dead homies.

Latrezz took a couple bites from his burger then sipped his drink. "Oh, what's wrong?"

"I don't know, I been under the weather all day." She responded.

"Well call me in the morning and let me know if you need anything." He added.

"Remember I have a doctor's appointment at 11:30." She reminded him.

"Oh yea, that's right. I'll be there in the morning." Latrezz was not accustomed to his new responsiblity as a father yet, but he was still excited.

"Okay, I'll see you in the morning, love you." She responded. Sometimes she worried but utimatley had faith that everything would work out. She had known Latrezz for years but they became serious after his acquittal.

"Love you too." Before Latrezz could even end the call, there were police lights flashing in his review mirror. He pulled over and rolled down his window. A white officer approached him.

"Is there a problem officer?" He casually asked the policeman.

"License and registration sir." The officer asked as he flashed his light into Latrezz' car.

Latrezz pulled a piece of paper out of his glove box and handed it to the officer. "Why am I being stopped?"

"Just sit tight." The officer said as he walked back to his patrol car with Latrezz' documents in hand. A white 90s Lincoln Town Car pulled behind the police car. Detective Walker steppped out and walked to Latrezz' window.

"What are you doing out at four o'clock in the morning?" Detective Walker questioned.

"Being black and minding my business. What's up?" Latrezz snapped.

Walker stood pointing his bright flashlight directly in Latrezz' eyes, "I'm goin' to need to search your vehicle."

"No your not. I have license, registration and insurance!" Latrezz felt confident challenging the officers because for all of the times that he was dirty, today he was clean.

"There's been a shooting in your neighborhood and you

look suspicious to me." Walker was determined on puttting Latrezz behind bars again.

"Look man I told you I'm not into all of that. I just left work." Latrezz' anger rose.

"Yea right. Now step out of the car." Walker placed his hand on the butt of his pistol.

"You can not legally search my car!" Latrezz snapped again.

"But I can search you and if you have *anything* you're going downtown." Latrezz stepped out of the car staring Walker directly in the eyes. Walker returned a sinister grin. The other officer knew this was harassment, but after all this was America where racism and prejudice among law enforcemnt was a custom.

The officer in uniform returned with Latrezz' paper work in his hand. He set it on the car then pat Latrezz down. "He's clean." The officer anounced.

"Are y'all done yet?" Latrezz questioned in an irrated tone of voice.

Walker's face turned to an angry sneer. "I will take your ass down if it's the last thing I do!" He stomped back to his vehicle as Latrezz rode away.

Less than a mile away, at the Interstate Bar & Grill, several members of the Alberta Gang mingled inside. JR sat at a table near the restroom sipping his drink. Every few minutes someone would summon him to the restroom, it was his cocaine office. He thought to himself about the fine young lady that he'd lost, then his mind thought about Tic and his other homies who'd recently been shot. JR felt a flash of anger pass through his whole body.

Outside, Taz stood near the bushes that were located across the street from the bar. Two black men in their twenties walked out of the bar. They surveyed the area with their eyes as one of them pulled out a blunt. Just as he lit it, Taz emerged from the bushes with a black Mac-11. Bullets sprayed out of the bulky gun. TTTTrrrraaatttt!!!! Both men collapsed, as they fell to the pavement the blood oozing from their wounds painted the cement red. Taz ran to the corner where an older modeled Buick Lesabre with its lights off was waiting. He hurried into the vehicle before it sped away into the night.

Larry was a slim black man in his forties who'd been in the neighborhood his whole life. He was no stranger to the thundering sound of gunshots, especially working here. He cautiously walked out of the club, wearing a food stained white apron over his clothes. He kneeled down to check the pulses of the two men. One Shot emerged from the bar coldy surveying the scene.

"Somebody get these boys some help. Call 911!!! Come on now damn it, these boys is dyin' out here!" Larry cried out.

One Shot pulled his cell phone out of his pocket then placed it in Larry's hand. Without saying a word he hopped into a gray Impala that was in the parking lot and drove away. A crowd of young black people poured out from the bar. About one third of the crowd was affiliated with the Alberta Gang, the rest consisted of hustlers who hung around the club and hood rats or gang bang groupies as some might call them. The sound of approaching sirens grew louder and louder. With all of the commotion, no one noticed what appeared to be a clown playing pool by himself in the empty bar.

Chapter 7

The next morning Mont and Cliff sat in their uncle's living room playing a violent video game. Latrezz entered the room smoking a blunt as he carried a glass of orange juice in his free hand. "What's up knuckleheads?" He called out to his nephews.

"What's up Uncle 'Trezz. Why are you up so early?" Cliff responded.

"Got to go handle some business." Latrezz replied as he passed his blunt to Cliff.

"Probably about to go do some square shit." Mont added as he jammed buttons on the controller in is hand.

"Oh you think so?" Latrezz asked grinning.

"Havin' a job and goin' to school don't make uncle 'Trezz a square it makes him responsible." Cliff added as he passed the blunt to his brother.

Mont took a long drag from the reefer filled cigar before replying. "And you a square for sayin' some weak ass shit like that."

Latrezz couldn't help but to laugh. His nephews didn't realize how much they reminded him of himself and Taz. "Yall tryin to make this run for me?" He asked shaking his head.

"Naw I was gettin' active last night I think I'm gon' play it safe until night time. I know I got one of 'em." Mont added casually.

Latrezz' facial expression quickly changed to furious as he turned his head toward the elder of his nephews. "I thought I told yo' hard headed ass to stay here!" His thunderous voice shook the room. Mont dropped his head to his chest. Latrezz began pacing aorund the room. "Damn nephew. Where yo' pistol at? We not about to have nothin' dirty sittin' over here. These mothafuckas followin' me and stoppin' me every chance they get, looking for a reason to take me back. DAMN NEPHEW! FUCK!"

Mont felt horrible about dissapointing his uncle. Deep down he just wanted to impress him. "Its in the closet." He said in a low tone.

Latrezz felt bad about yelling at his nephew, but now he truly understood his sister's frustration with the boys. "Well you can still go. My white homegirl is on her way to take yall to Tillamook to pick up two P's. Y'all not gon' need no heat down there."

"I say better safe then sorry. If we get stopped with two Pz and a white bitch on I-5 we done anyway." Mont added as he passed the blunt to his uncle.

"Naw smart ass, she has a medical marijuana card. I'm just sendin' y'all to watch my money…" He took a long drag from the blunt. "And don't try to rob her Mont."

"Well the bitch better not slip!" Mont jested his uncle, causing Cliff to chuckle.

"Keep fuckin' with me and it's gon' be me and you!" Latrezz stiffly poked Mont in the chest then walked to the closet to grab the pistol. He closed the closet then walked out the door.

In his uncles's absense, Mont spoke up. "Damn, Uncle Trezz be actin like a bitch sometimes." Cliff just shook his head, he knew it was useless to start a debate with his brother.

Latrezz walked to his car and opened the trunk. He placed Cliff's gun under the spare tire before shutting the trunk and driving away. As he rode toward his woman's house, he couldn't help but too think what could happen if Walker stopped him right now.

All morning long Walker and his cop buddies had been engaged in a chavinistic group text conversation. They shared GIFs with their colleagues about Obama, police brutality and oddly black porn. Deep down the heinous officers lusted the provacative young women who lived on their turf. Once a year they took a trip to Las Vegas to gamble and order prostitutes who traveled from Portland. After the deed was done instead of paying the officers would threaten to arrest the young women.

"FUCK!" Latrezz exclaimed.

Sandy looked over toward Latrezz and grabbed his hand. "What's wrong baby? Are you okay?"

"Everything is cool. I think this asshole detective is followin' me though." He responded trying to be cool.

"So what? You don't have anything to hide you've been on a straight narrow for along time now. Plus you have responsibility now its absolutely no way you could get caught up in that shit again…. Right?" Sandy couldn't understand why he was so upset.

Latrezz hesitated as he thought about the dirty pistol that was in his trunk. "Yea that's right."

Inside the hospital lobby dozens of people walked or navigated wheel chairs to their destinations. Walker approached the receptionist desk.

"How may I help you sir?" The chubby white receptionist asked as she smiled at the detective.

"How are you doing today? I'm Detective Walker with the Portland Police Department. I'm investigating a double shooting that happened early this morning. The victims were brought here by ambulance." Walker responded.

"One moment detective." The receptionist picked up the telephone and dialed a number. After a brief conversation she returned her attention to Walker. "Go to the seventh floor intensive care unit."

"Thanks" Walker replied. He walked to the elevator and pressed the up button. After only a few moments the doors opened and he stepped inside.

Once the elevator door closed, Latrezz and Sandy entered the lobby. They approached the receptionist desk. "Hello. How may I help you?" The receptionist asked.

"I have an appointment with Dr. Butler." Sandy responded.

"Go to the sixth floor and make a left off of the elevator. His office is right there." The receptionist informed the young couple.

"Thank you." Sandy replied as she and Latrezz walked to the elevator.

Inside the elevator Sandy broke the silence. "Are you prepared to be a father? Be honest."

Latrezzed paused. "I think so."

"Don't think I'm going to need you to know, because if you're not we can consider other options." Latrezz hated when Sandy became worked up like this.

"What other options? We conceived a child and now we have a responsibility to raise that child." He responded.

Sandy cried as she spoke. "I'm just sayin' I can't do this alone Latrezz."

Latrezz gently wiped Sandy's tears away with his thumbs. "Do you trust me?"

"Of course but-"

"But nothin'." He cut her off mid sentence. "If you trust me then take my word. I'll be there."

She looked toward Latrezz with tears in her eyes. "Promise?"

"Promise," Latrezz replied, then kissed his woman on the foredhead.

Meanwhile, in the ICU, Larry sat in a chair next to a crying black woman as Walker spoke with a nurse near the window. "There was another shooting victim that came in earlier last night also." She informed him.

"Do you think the incidents are related?" Walker asked.

"I don't know you're the detective." The nurse replied then handed a folded piece of paper to Walker. He placed the paper in his pocket and nodded at the nurse.

"These are dangerous people that we're dealing with." He informed her.

"Well hopefully you guys can get it under control. I doubt it if either of these guys make it through the week." The nurse added.

"Hopefully they hurry up and croak so I can do this paper work." Walker grinned at the nurse. She found his comments to be chilling so she quietly walked away.

"Fuck you peckawood mothafucka!!!" Larry stood up and approached Walker. "Those are human beings in there!"

"And how many other human beings have they shot up in their life time? Two less nutty motherfuckers running around here if you ask me." Walker stated coldly.

"I knew both of those boys since they were little. Those was good people. What if that was your family layin in there." Larry asked.

Walker still lacked empathy, "Nobody in my family

would be hanging out in that shit hole of a bar during a gang war."

"Go to hell punk mothafucka!" Larry ordered.

"After you... BROTHA!" Walker replied coldly.

On the sixth floor, Latrezz and Sandy stood in front of the receptionist desk. This receptionist was a young almond complexioned woman who wore glasses.

"Okay all I need is your insurance cards and the doctor will be out to see you shortly." The receptionist announced.

Sandy fumbled through her purse. "Damn it, I must've left it in the car."

"It's cool baby, I'll go get it for you." Latrezz assured his woman.

"Okay just bring it to me and I'll direct you to the room she's in." The receptionist advised him.

"Please don't take forever." Sandy whined as Latrezz walked back to the elevator.

Latrezz walked through the parking lot until he reached his car. After sitting down on the driver's side, he opened his glove department then grabbed a stack of envelopes. After hearing the sound of loud music fill the air, he curiously looked up. In the reflection of his rear view mirror, he spotted a white 2007 Entrepid park in the row behind him. Once the music stopped, One Shot, Randall and another young black man exited the entrepid. All of the men cautiously looked over their shoulders in every direction.

"Punk ass One Shot!" Latrezz said out loud.

Latrezz thought back to the summer when he was 16. At that time One Shot was known for turning out most of the

Killingsworth functions. He recalled one parrticular party when a young One Shot hopped out of his 1987 brown Caprice and opened fire on a crowd of Killingsworth Street gangsters. BANG! BANG! BANG! That shooting left two of his friends wounded.

Later, that same year, a young Taz and Latrezz bailed down the street wearing dark blue hoodies and beanies. They were on their way to the weed man's house.

"You think this shit gon be some fire?" Latrezz asked. "Last time Tiny had some straight swap."

"Well either way I already told him he gon have to light some of that shit up if he want me to fuck with the whole zip. And the most I'm droppin is two." Taz said in a matter of fact tone.

"Yea and if he got a problem with that I'm down to just take that shit on the set." The brothers were silent as they made eye contact with each other.

"Yea if he on that bullshit I'm wit it." Taz spoke up.

About half a block ahead, One Shot's brown Caprice was parked with smoke rising out of the windows. Inside One shot sat in the driver seat wearing a beanie with a white "A" on it. His little brother Stevie sat in the passenger seat wearing a gray hoodie. They passed reefer back and forth as they zoned out to the music.

Taz and Latrezz continued down the street. "What's up with them bitches from the other day? The dark skinned one was THHHHHICCCCCK!" Latrezz said with his fist in his hand. Taz stopped in his tracks and put his arm out blocking Latrezz from walking.

Taz squinted and slightly leaned to the side. "A there go

that brown Caprice."

Latrezz looked up the street and noticed One Shot's car parked with smoke rising out of the slightly cracked windows. Latrezz reached into his pocket. "Fuck that!!!"

Taz held out his arm. "Hold up I don't think they see us."

"So why we not blastin yet?" Latrezz asked, pistol in hand.

"Would you rather walk or run?" Taz asked.

The brothers approached the Caprice slowly with their hoods and gloves on. One Shot passed the blunt to Stevie. The inside of the car was so cloudy, they could barely see in front of themselves. Stevie took a long drag from the blunt. Just as he coughed, the sound of loud gunshots and shattering glass overtook the music as bullets flew through the car.

Latrezz and Taz stood about three feet from One Shot's car shooting into it. Several bullet holes gaped in the ceiling and walls of the car. The side windows were completely shot out. Shattered glass and smoke could be seen in the light that peaked through the bullet holes.

One Shot leaned over and cradled his brother. Stevie's hoodie was soaked with blood. His hands shook uncontrollably. His right hand still held a burning blunt with blood dripping off the end of it. One Shot sped away, his vehicle followed by bullets as he fled the scene.

Back at the hospital, Latrezz watched as One Shot walked into the entrance of the hospital followed by Randall and the other man. Latrezz walked to his trunk and retrieved his nephew's pistol. He looked around as he slid it into his pocket, then closed the trunk. Even though it had been close to a decade since Stevie was shot, he still couldn't afford to take any chances.

When Latrezz entered the lobby of the hospital again, One Shot and company stood waiting in front of the elevator. Latrezz made a sharp right and entered the stairwell next to the elevator. He was so quick the other men never noticed him walking only five feet behind them.

Once inside the elevator, Randall spoke up, "This shit is fucked up cuddy. I'm gon kill one of them niggas."

"Its far from over." One Shot assured, "Lil Bro comin' home today and I got to fill him in on all this bullshit. Its on sight whenever and where ever I bump into *ANY* of them niggas. On Big Tic."

Meanwhile, Latrezz walked up the stairwell pass the door that read "4". He heard the creeking of the heavy door opening. Walker entered the stairwell through the door that read "7" as he talked on a cell phone.

"No suspects yet in this case but these guys are pretty much done for. I just found a lead on a sixteen year old kid that was shot in the leg last night. We need to keep our eyes on the Tillmans. I know what they're capable of and I'm sure that the young ones are following in their uncles' footsteps." Walker's voice startled Latrezz. He exited the stairwell through the door that read "5".

Sandy sat on a hospital bed wearing a patient's gown. Dr. Butler was a clean cut light complexioned man in his late 20s. He stood in front of Sandy with a clipboard in his hand. Latrezz entered the room sweating and panting.

"What took you so long? Why are you out of breath?"

Sandy medaled.

"Took the stairs, tryin to stay fit." Latrezz fought to get the words out as he gasped for breath. Sandy cracked a grin at Latrezz.

Once the appointment was over, Latrezz and Sandy walked back to Latrezz' car.

"Are you excited?" She asked.

"Hell yea!" He put his arm around her waist. "From this point on the only people in the world are you and my child.

At that exact moment, One Shot, Randall and the other man emerged from the hospital. The trio frowned and walked hard toward the parking lot. Latrezz spotted them and gently shoved Sandy toward the car.

"Come on baby get in the car." Latrezz said anxiously.

"Okay," She replied in an irritated tone. Once inside, Latrezz impatiently looked over his shoulder. "You want to get somethin to eat?" She asked.

"Yea we can do that." Latrezz responded.

One Shot and company stopped at the trunk of their car. "Fuck that! I'm ready right now!" Randall spoke up.

"How the fuck am I gon' tell grandma we got to plan another funeral and Tic aint even buried yet? FUCK!" One Shot asked to no one in paticular.

Latrezz watched the trio through his rear view mirror and slowly reached into his pocket.

"Did you forget something?" Sandy asked.

"Naw, we about to be on our way." He replied, never taking his eyes off of his rear view mirror. When Sandy looked at Latrezz she noticed the gun on his lap. She followed his dazed glare to the rear view mirror.

"Damn it Latrezz! What's goin on? Who the fuck is that?" Her voice shrieked.

"What?" Latrezz looked at his woman, then back to the rear view mirror. "Naw aint nothing goin on baby. Just be cool."

Sandy stared angrily ahead as she crossed her arms. "This is bullshit!"

Finallly, the car full of Alberta street gangsters drove away. Latrezz' car pulled out and drove in the opposite direction.

Sandy sat with her arms crossed. "What the hell was that about? Please don't tell me you're getting caught up in the streets again." He knew it was only a matter of time before She would break the awkward silence.

"Naw-" before he could get the words out the sound of screeching tires cut him off. Walker's car pulled directly in Latrezz' path. "Fuck!" Latrezz exclaimed.

Walker exited his car abruptly then approached Latrezz' car. Latrezz and Sandy looked at each other without saying a word as Walker knocked on Latrezz' window.

Latrezz rolled his window about a 1/4 down. "What's up?"

"Get out of the car asshole." Walker ordered.

"For what?" Latrezz asked sounding irritated.

"Why are you up here?" Walker questioned.

"My girl is pregnant man. Damn!" he replied.

"Let's go Nut!" Walker ordered!

Latrezz stepped out of the car and placed his hands on the hood. He knew that if Walker found that gun he was going to jail. Sandy smacked her gums.

"You too baby mama drama." Walker motioned the young woman out of the car. Sandy stepped out of the car belly first. She held her purse in one hand and a bottle of water in the other, occasionally taking sips.

Walker pat Latrezz down then stopped briefly. "One wrong move asshole! One wrong move!" Walker looked toward Sandy. She smiled at him in return.

"For such a handsome officer you sure don't smile a lot." She flirted causing Walker to blush.

"And for such a pretty girl you sure don't keep good company." He replied. Even though she was visibly pregrant, any man would've been powerless to the attractive young woman's smile.

"Well if you don't mind I really have to potty." She announced in a whiny voice.

Latrezz and Walker stared each other down, both men's eyes revealed a deep mutual hatred. "Okay, I'm goin to let you go on your way." Walker said. Just as Latrezz started to open his door, Walker spoke up. "Let me take a look under your seats first."

Walker ducked into Latrezz' car peering under the seats. Sandy swayed from side to side as she wiped sweat from her face. Finally, Walker emerged from the car. He looked toward Sandy. "Okay get out of here."

Latrezz and Sandy quietly drove away. Sandy angrily stared straight ahead. She reached into her purse and pulled the gun out then placed it on Latrezz' lap.

"I appreciate that." He spoke up.

"Just drive motherfucker! " she snapped.

Katie and the boys drove for over two hours smoking weed and listening to reggae. Mont lit a blunt, took a long drag then coughed violently. "The ganja too hardcore for you?" Katie asked smiling

Mont beat on his chest then replied in a very dry voice. "Its aight. I just hit it too hard."

"That shit smell like some power." Cliff added.

"Here's the exit." Katie announced as she pulled off of the freeway. They made their way through a heavily wooded area and turned down a gravel road. Katie parked near a wooden cabin about five miles off of the main road. Mont and Cliff curiously gazed around as they exited the car.

"Hope you guys are ready for a little nature walk. It's about a mile into the woods." Katie announced in a bubbly voice.

"Damn, what happened to the days of buying weed on M.L.K.?" Mont asked in a sarcastic voice.

Cliff chuckled, "Shut up fool."

"Well before it gets to M.L.K. somebody has to pick it up from here." Katie added.

When they reached the end of their hike, an older Mexican man and a teen aged Mexican boy both wearing gardening gloves stood near two Earth toned brendal pit bulls.

"There she is." The older man said smiling. "Who are your buddies?"

"Hey Hector, they're totally cool. " Katie assured him smiling ear to ear.

Cliff squinted. "Juan?"

Juan reached in to shake Cliff's hand. "Cliff! What's up homes? How's it goin?"

"Pretty good. I haven't seen you since the eighth grade. Where you been at?"" Cliff asked in an excited tone.

"Right here. I been tryin to make this money fuck school." Juan informed his old school buddy.

"You still got a plug on thangs?" Cliff inquired.

"Always. Take my number homes." Juan added.

Hector reached into a large black trash bag and pulled out two large zip lock bags full of marijuana. He handed the bags to Katie. She immediately placed the bags in her back pack. Mont pulled a small brown paper bag out of his hoody pocket and handed it to Hector.

CHAPTER 8

Mrs. Tillman sat at the end of her couch eating fruit out of a clear plastic container. Retha sat at the other end as they watched a court show. Before she rose from her seat, Retha knew that the heavy knock on the door was her little brother Taz.

"Well look at what the devil dragged in." Retha said at the sight of her little brother.

"Shut up." Taz snapped back at his sister.

"So you finally decided to give your poor old Mammy a visit huh? I almost forgot I had a son." Mrs. Tillman teased.

Taz grinned as he leaned over to give his mother a hug and a kiss on the cheek. Mrs. Tillman grinned back at her son. "I was comin by to let you know I'm about to go down to Vegas for a week or so Mama."

Mrs. Tillman cocked her eyebrows up. "Vegas huh? What you goin down there for? "

"Just to get away for a second." Taz replied casually.

"You takin Kisha" She asked.

"No, Mama" Taz replied.

"What are you tryin to get away from?" Ms. Tillman asked.

"I just need a little break is all." He couldn't look his mother in the eyes.

"Yea right." Retha added.

Mrs. Tillman took her attention off of the T.V., "When are you goin to grow up boy? You aint foolin nobody but yourself you act just like your Daddy used to. You know he used to flirt with death too and that's why he's dead now. When you comin back to church?"

Taz dropped his head to his chest. As hard as he

was, he still felt like a little boy when his mother spoke to him like this. "Once I get back I'll go to church with you."

"Don't do it for me, do it for yourself." Mrs. Tillman lectured.

"Okay Mama." Taz said holding back a tear. He wanted to cry in his mother's arms, but that wasn't what being a gangster was about.

"Where's your brother and your big head nephews at?" Mrs. Tillman inquired.

"I spoke to 'em this morning. I think Trezz had to take Sandy to the doctor today." Taz added.

"And where are my sons at? I told they bad asses to be over here!" Retha was upset because she had not spoke to them since the previous morning.

Taz cracked a wide grin. "Damn you need to keep up with your rugrats sis."

"Shut up Taz!" She snapped.

Taz kept chuckling the same way he did as a little boy. He cheesed ear to ear as he pulled his phone out of his pocket. "Excuse me Mama. I'm gon take this call outside." He walked outside holding his phone to his ear. Taz immediately noticed the white Entrepid slowly creeping in front of his Mom's house. His eyes grew wide as he reached into his pocket.

BANG! BANG! BANG! Mrs. Tillman and Retha ducked on the ground covering their heads, as bullets pierced the walls. After hearing the sound of screeching tires, Mrs. Tillman and Retha bolted onto the porch. They foundTaz laying in a pool of his own blood gasping for breath. Still holding his nickel plated .357 in his right hand.

Mrs. Tilmman dropped to her knees and cradled Taz' head. Retha just stared into the distance as if in a daze. "Hold on baby… Just hold on… Lord please don't take my baby from me…." Mrs. Tillman said as she rocked back and forth weeping.

A few blocks away Mont and Cliff stopped at the corner store for blunts and juice. They left the store in the direction of their Grandmother's house. Mont looked down the empty street. "Aint nobody even out here. Who want to fuck with us little bro?"

Cliff cracked a grin, "Lets get to Grandma's house so we can light that shit up mayne."

At the same moment, One Shot was speeding away from the crime scene he'd just created. "There go Mont right there. He popped the homie last night. Them is ol' boy's nephews." Randall said.

"Well now its time for some get back little cuddy," Stevie spoke up.

"Bitch ass niggas." One Shot added.

Stevie and Randall jumped out of the car and approached Mont and Cliff on foot. Mont pulled a knife out of his pocket at the sight of his rivals.

"Fuck! They probably strapped." He cursed.

"So what you tryin to do?" Cliff asked.

"They want me. You just go home little bro. Get the homies." Mont ordered.

"I'm not leavin you." Cliff stood his ground.

Stevie and Randall stopped within arms reach of Mont and Cliff. "What that Murda block like?" Stevie called out.

"I'm on this Killingsworth shit loc!" Mont responded.

Stevie pulled a rusty black .38 Special out of his waist band and opened fire. Each crackeling shot roaring like thunder. Simultaneously, Randall also let off a few shots in the boy's direction with his pocket rocket. Stevie and Randall ran back to One Shot's car. The white Entrepid smashed off, leaving the young brothers on the cold sidewalk in a puddle of blood. Mont's hands cradled Cliff's head. As Cliff floated away, he gazed down and thought to himself, "Damn I can't get caught in these scuffed ass Chucks."

Meanwhile at Big Sherm's house, Big Sherm played cards with Black.

"Get on some of this wet Nut." Sherm offered.

"Naw brotha. I'm cool." Latrezz responded as he examined an assault rifle. His phone began to ring. The longer he held the phone to his ear, the more his facial expression became confused. "Yea.... What? When?.... where?... Fuck! Did you see who it was?"

Big Sherm slowly shuffled cards as he looked up toward Latrezz. He knew something was wrong when Latrezz' phone dropped as he stared blankly into space.

"Everythang aight?" Big Sherm asked.

"Naw the brands just tore up Taz at my Mama's house." Latrezz said with a blank expression on his face.

Black slammed his cards down and jumped up. "What?!"

"Black round up all the homies. I'm callin a meeting tonight." Sherm announced.

"On me Nut I'll handle that shit for you homie. Don't even trip." Black assured his childhood friend.

"Yea we pullin' out the big thangs tonight!" Big Sherm said in a husky voice.

Several teenagers gathered in the lobby of the emergency room. Mrs. Tillman, Retha and Kisha wept near the patient hallway entrance. Baby Stomp sat in the corner of the room talking quietly with a small group of Killingsworth gang members. Cookie sat with her cousin's crying.

Latrezz entered the room with his head down and walked toward his mother. "What happened?" he asked.

Retha threw a set of wild punches at Latrezz. "Where were you? You were supposed to keep 'em safe!" She cried out between sobs.

Latrezz caught Retha's hands then restrained her with a hug. "Sis… Sis…" Retha cried in Latrezz' arms. He looked up and saw his Mom wiping tears from her eyes with a hankerchief.

"They got your nephews Latrezz." She informed him.

A tear fell from Latrezz' eye. "What?" He asked as his voice cracked. At that very moment Latrezz felt the ground crumble beneath his feet. He couldn't understand why his world had to be in shambles all the time. Three steps ahead, five steps back. He tried hard to change but the universe just wouldn't let Nut go.

Mont opened his eyes and observed the small dark room with dry erase boards on the wall. He gazed curiously at the I.V. and vital monitor connected to his arm. Mont shivered, he had never felt this cold in his young life.

A nurse pressed a button on the vital monitor. "How

are you feeling?" she asked.

"Where's my little brother?" Mont asked groggily.

The nurse opened the blinds. "Just relax. Do you need anything?"

Mont sat up. "Where is my brother at?" He repeated.

The nurse hesitated, "I'm sorry Lamont, we couldn't save him."

Mont violently jumped up then instantly collapsed. He cried at the top of his lungs, "MUTHAFUCKAS!!!"

Meanwhile, at One Shot's house, the Murda Gang congregated. Several young black men sported baseball caps or beanies with A's on them. Randall played with a pit bull puppy on the floor, while Stevie lifted weights on the excercise bench. One Shot sat on the couch chopping crack with a razor blade. He wrapped each small chunk in plastic.

"You know while I was sittin down its one thing I thought about everyday." Stevie said as he pushed the weights up.

"What's that?" One Shot asked.

"Well of course all of my old bitches..." Stevie replied, causing Randall to snicker. "But on the real though, I dreamt it out in my head every day. Goin to see Nut's bitch ass and takin him off the set!"

"I haven't saw or heard about him since he caught that case." One Shot spoke up.

"I thought he beat that?" Stevie inquired.

"Me too, but I still haven't seen him though." One Shot responded.

"The homies told me he was at the school pickin' up his bitch ass nephews after we smashed on 'em the other day." Randall was anxious to provide info on the situation.

"Well let's do it." One Shot endorsed the mission.

110 Stevie stopped lifting and sat up. "I'm with that."

The scene at Big Sherm's house was almost identical to One Shot's. Several young black men gathered in the basement, Most of them sported baseball caps or beanies with Ks on them. Some of them smoked dodi while others dipped cigarettes in sherm.

Latrezz sat silently on the couch next to Big Sherm as he took drags off of a cigarette. "I know how you feel Nut. I remember when the brands took my bro in '93. Me and Big Shady loaded our heats, lit some sherm and hit the streets... When the smoke cleared like twenty of them niggas was lickin their wounds and seven was dead.... That's over the course of a month. Shit that's how I got my name." Latrezz turned toward Big Sherm. Now that he knew he had Latrezz' attention he continued. "The hood is in your hands right now. It's your call. What you wanna do?"

"Let me get some of that wet." Latrezz asked.

Blig Sherm stood up and walked to the back of the room. Latrezz' phone started to vibrate. It read: Sandy. He pushed the ignore button and stood up. "From here on out don't contact me unless its about a 187. If you want to kick back I understand. But if you representin' this shit we gon do it to the full." Latrezz announced.

"Fuck Aberta! Let's get on their heads!" One of the gangsters yelled out. Big Sherm returned grinning with a sherm stick in his hand. He handed it to Latrezz who then lit it and took a deep drag.

The room began to spin causing Latrezz to feel dizzy. A small clown appeared on the couch next to Latrezz. He chuckled in a creepy high pitched tone. After what felt like a blink of an eye, Latrezz found himself riding down the street with his homies.

Big Sherm's black Impala cruised down the street. "Uh-oh, what do we have here." He asked rhetorically.

A high pitched shrieking chuckle interupted the trance Latrezz was in. He lifted his head and looked out the window. A young black man wearing a baseball cap with an "A" on it walked down the street.

A short shadowy figure walked behind the man. The obnoxious chuckling in Latrezz' ear began to agitate him. He pointed his gun out the window, then lowered it as he attempted to make out the shadowy figure on the sidewalk behind the young man.

BANG! BANG! BANG! Shots rang out as the man collapsed.

"Hold up," Latrezz ordered as he stepped out of the car.

"What the fuck? What are you doin Nut? We need to go." Black yelled from the backseat.

Latrezz could still hear the creepy high pitched chuckling echoing in streets, drowning out the sound of a million rain drops splashing on the grimy concrete. He slowly stepped onto the sidewalk with his gun in hand. The injured man crawled up the sidewalk moaning and groaning in an attempt to escape.

"Latrezz," The high pitched voice echoed.

The injured man desperately attempted to aim his gun at Latrezz. Before he could steady himself, a small banana yellow Chuck Taylor, kicked the gun away. Before he could react the smalll foot kicked the injured man violently in the head. Latrezz' eyes grew big.

"Come on Nut! Hurry up we got to go!" Black called out.

A short clown with a demonic grin stood at the injured man's head. A red bolt of lightning fell from the sky, striking the blunt in the clowns mouth. He took a long drag, burning the half of the cigar in one pull. When he exhaled, the smoke from his lungs filled the streets with a thick fog. "I'll put the work in for you homie." The clown said as he began to chuckle.

The clown unbuttoned his pants then a stream of liquid poured on the injured man's head as he attempted to crawl away. "Want to see something funny?" The clown asked still chuckling. He dropped the lit blunt on the injured man's wet head. The liquid on the man's head and upper body caught fire. The flames illuminated the pale demonic grin. The chuckling grew louder as the injured man groaned painfully.

"Let's go!" Latrezz ordered as he jumped into the car. He wasn't sure what he had just seen as the vehicle sped away.

"Still crazy then a mothafucka, that's for sure." Big Sherm thought out loud.

"I think I saw the devil back there." Latrezz spoke truthfully.

Big Sherm chuckled, "I bet you did."

Latrezz shifted his vision to the rear view mirror. The evil clown threw up the Killingsworth gang sign. Latrezz shook his head and rubbed his eyes.

"Nut? You cool what you lookin at?" Black asked, his voice eched and sounded deep like it had been chopped and screwed.

When Latrezz looked out the window the clown stood over the flaming carcass on the dark street. The creepy high pitched chuckling felt like it was in Latrezz' ear. He was sweating profusely. Latrezz turned around only to find the clown was in the back seat next to Black.

"I told you I got yo back. Fuck them Alberta niggas." The clown said with a twisted smile on his face. Now Latrezz felt the inside of the car spinning like a merigo-round from hell. He'd never felt this dizzy before and everything was so fucking blurry.

Big Sherm's deep chuckles grew more faint with each sound. Black sounded like he was under water as he called out "Nut…. Nut…"

"Yea you handled that." Latrezz said out loud. The clown responded with more high pitched chuckling.

The inside of the car stopped spinning. "Nut?" Black called out.

Latrezz sat up and wiped sweat from his face. "What's up?"

"Who you talkin' to?" Black asked with a confused look on his face.

"HUH?" Latrezz responded sounding even more confused.

"You cool?" Black asked.

"Yea I'm straight homie." Latrezz responded in sync with the bizzarre clown.

That night Latrezz could not sleep. When he finally dozed off he dreamt about his child being born. There he was at the hospital with his arms out as the doctor handed him the small infant who was swaddled in a blanket. When he moved the blanket to look the baby in the eyes, he revealed the face of that hideous clown and the cries turned to creepy chuckling. Latrezz jumped out up out of his sleep in a cold sweat.

Latrezz sat on his bed fully clothed, still wearing the dark hoody, beanie and gloves from the night before. He held a half empty bottle of liquor as tears ran down his cheeks. Brandy walked up and licked his face. He pet her on the head, then stood up and exited the room.

Latrezz held a large gun in his right hand and a bag of dog food in his left hand. He stopped at the front door amd cocked his gun. He slowly opened the door then looked around in every direction before stepping outside.

Brandy and Taz' puppy followed Latrezz into the back yard. He poured food into two small chrome bowls in the corner of the yard then picked up two more empty bowls and filled them with water. The pit bulls' heads were buried in the bowls as they scarfed down food. The back yard was filled with the sounds of dog smacking, crunching and heavy breathing. Latrezz placed the bowls of water next to the bowls with food in them. The dogs quickly removed their heads from the empty bowls to quench their thirst, rapidly splashing their tongues into the water.

Latrezz walked down the street mumbling holding both leashes in one hand. "The audassity of these mothafuckas to fuck with me and mines. I don't think they know what they got themselves into. Yesterday I was on a mission to do better. Today I don't give a fuck about nothin' but getting back at these fools."

Latrezz walked up to his Mother's porch with Brandy and the younger dog. He tied their leashes around a chair on the porch then knocked on the door. He couldn't help but to notice his brother's dried up blood on the floor and several bullet holes in front of the house.

"Who Is it?" Mrs. Tillman asked.

"Its me Mama." Latrezz resonded.

She slowly opened the door and looked up at Latrezz. Her watery eyes told the graphic narrative of the grief that millions of black mothers in America felt from losing a child in the streets. Latrezz hugged her tightly, he couldn't control the tears rolling down his cheeks.

"Come on in baby." She said.

Once Latrezz walked in, Mrs. TIllman pulled the door shut behind him. Retha sat on the couch crying. She wiped her tears with a tissue. Latrezz dropped his head to his chest. "I'm sorry sis."

"You aint got nothin' to be sorry about." She wiped tears from her face "You not them boys daddy. I just don't know how... where I went wrong. It just seem like they listen to y'all more then me."

Latrezz grabbed his sister's hand. "I promise you its not over."

"Don't talk like that boy. Vengeance is the Lord's. Don't you forget that." Mrs. Tillman advised her youngest child.

"But how can I just let that go Mama? My brother and my nephew." he cired out.

"Think about your baby." Her voice shattered as crocodile tears covered her puffy cheeks.

"My child will be taken care of." Latrezz spoke up.

"You're going to have to be big enough to swallow your pride and let it go. Remember your life is in God's hands. Don't let the devil tempt you to be evil. Its okay to feel angry, but when you let that anger enter your heart and control you it will destroy you." She couldn't help but to lecure her son. She knew that he was hurting and confused, but she figured that as long as he stayed rooted in Jesus he would be alright.

Latrezz nodded. "Well I'm goin to get out of here Mama."

"You don't want nothin' to eat? I got some food in there." She desparately wanted him to stay with her. She feared whatever he was so anxious to get back to.

"I'm not hungry." He said as he walked out on to the porch. He began to untie the dogs.

Retha stepped out of the house behind Latrezz. "You walked over here?" She asked.

"Yea. I needed some fresh air." He responded as he started down the stairs.

"Stevie's out." Retha blurted.

Latrezz stopped in his tracks, then turned toward Retha. "Where did you hear that?"

"I didn't hear it no where. Stevie and One Shot killed Taz." she responded coldly.

The sound of thunder rumbled the ground as lightning cracked the sky. Rain began pouring down. Latrezz' twisted his face. His eyes glowed furious burning red.

"The detective said at least one of the guns was used in both shootings." Retha added.

He looked his sister in her eyes, his face was dripping wet from rain and tears. She returned his stare, tears ran down her face as well.

"I'll handle it." He assured his sister as he lead the dogs onto the side walk. Retha stood on the porch crying while her Mother watched from behind the screen door.

Latrezz was dripping wet as he walked the dogs down a rainy street. When he reached his house, Sandy stood on the porch ringing the door bell.

"Oh my God!" Her hands flew to her mouth, "You're all wet. Why are you walking in the rain?" Latrezz looked at Sandy briefly then continued to the front door of the house. She followed him inside.

"I heard what happened baby. I just want to let you know that I'm here for you. I been callin you back to back. If you want to talk I'm here." She assured him in an empathetic tone of voice.

"I don't feel like talking," he coldy responded.

"Do you need anything? You hungry?" she asked.

"I just need to be alone right now." His voice was emotionless and Sandy could barely recognize the man she was starting a family with.

"As long as I'm here you'll never be alone." She paused. "Remember what you promised me?"

"I'll be there." He asured her.

Sandy walked to the linen closet and pulled a towel out. She walked back toward Latrezz holding the towel out unfolded. "Come here,"

Latrezz lowered his head as Sandy used the towel to dry him off. Once his face was dry she kissed him on the cheek. She held his wrists and looked in his eyes, he returned an emotionless gaze.

"Let's move away and start over." She pleaded.

"I been here my whole life why should I move? Not for these bitch ass niggas. Hell naw!" He raged.

Sandy dropped her head to her chest. "I'm scared Latrezz."

"Don't be." he attempted to sound sane. "Just give me some time to get my mind right baby."

At Emanuel Hospital several teenagers sat around the emergency lobby waiting for any updates on Mont's condition. Mrs. Tillman, Retha and Cookie wept near the patient hallway entrance. Mont slowly limped out of a hallway assisted by a nurse.

The nurse held a white paper bag in her hand with writing on it. "Make sure you take these atleast twice a day. I would recommend that you stay in bed for at least a week." Mont nodded at the nurse. " We really prefer that you stay a little longer, your body is still trying to recover."

Mont ignored the nurse and walked into his mother's arms. A river of tears flowed freely down his cheeks.

"I love you," She expressed to her last living seed. She couldn't remember the last time she said those words to him.

"I love you too Mama." He replied.

"You ready to go home baby?" She asked.

"Its not safe for y'all to be around me right now Mama. Let me stay with Uncle Taz until things calm down I don't want to pull Uncle 'Trezz into this." He was not aware of his uncle's condition. Retha started sobbing

Mrs. Tillman wiped tears from her eyes with a handkerchief, then placed her hand on Mont's back. "Your Uncle Tasir is dead baby." She informed her grandson.

A tear fell from Mont's eye. "What? Grandma no!" Mont felt himself freeze as if he was caught in Medusa's glare.

"I'm so sorry baby." Mrs. Tillman added.

Lamont noticed Cookie for the first time, she was standing off to the side. She rushed up to him and hugged him. "I'm so scared baby, I don't want to lose you." She cried out.

"I'm too hot right now baby, I think it would be best if we took a break. I don't want to put you in harm's way." He responded.

"Move to Oklahoma with me Lamont, I can't be without you." She pleaded.

"When shit get right we can work on us, but right now I need you to stay away from me." Mont and Cookie both experienced the unbearable feeling of their hearts shattering into a billion peices. She sobbed as her cousin's led her outside. Mont didn't want to let her go, but right now was not the time to for romance, murder was on the menu.

Meanwhile, at Swan Island, Dennis sat in is office flipping through paperwork until he found Latrezz' file. The walls of his office were filled with dry erase boards, calendars and posters. The television in the front of the room cut to a breaking news story.

"There have been several shootings over the past week. Last night a man was found shot on the side walk. His upper body was burned to a crisp. Forensic scientists are trying to figure out what chemical was used to burn the man. There are no leads in the case." Dennis barely paid the news anchor on the T.V. screen any attention.

He picked up the phone and dialed Latrezz' number. "Hello," Latrezz answered from the other end of the phone line.

"Hey Latrezz its Dennis. How are you doing this morning?" Dennis asked in a gruff sounding voice.

"What's up Dennis. Honestly, not that well." Latrezz responded honestly.

"I was calling to discuss the full time position if you were still interested. But if this isn't a good time I can always call back or wait until you come in tonight."

"Well I do need and want that position. But I need to take some time off both my brother and nephew were killed. I need some time to grieve." Latrezz said as he examined the pistol in his hand.

Dennis didn't know how to respond. He paused for a moment then continued. "Oh I'm sorry to hear that. I'll tell you what, take a few weeks off then call me when your ready and I'll get you goin'."

"Thank you," Latrezz replied.

"No problem. Its not every day that we come across

employees as reliable as you." Dennis added.

Latrezz hung up the phone. He could still hear distant chuckling. He sat at his coffee table and began to break down a sticky bud of marijuana. He pulled a cigar out of his pocket, split it down the middle with his thumbs and dumped the tobacco out. He then filled the empty shell with the marijuana and rolled it.

Latrezz stood up and exited the room. His bedroom was full of empty alcohol bottles and plastic bags. Next to the alarm clock on the night stand was a black lighter and a bottle of Hennessy. As he reached for the Hennessy the lighter fell to the floor then landed next to a black jar.

He walked back into his living room with the bottle in one hand and the lighter in the other then took a seat on the couch. As he smoked the blunt he never took his eyes off of the jar. He put it out about half way through then picked the jar up.

Latrezz opened the jar and took a wif, he inhaled the foul stench. Still he dipped the tip of the blunt into the jar. He lit it again and took a deep drag. He heard the creepy chuckling again. Brandy cocked her head at Latrezz. The clown entered the room grinning demonically. He appeared to be slightly taller.

The clown pet Brandy, in return she whimpered and exited the room. "What's up Nut?" His chilling voice was slightly deeper.

Latrezz hesitated then asked, "Who the in the hell are you?"

"Well technically I'm not in hell but I am of hell." the clown chuckled, "Get it?!"

"What do you want with me?" Latrezz asked.

"I am you." The clown took a swig of alcohol. "You been keepin' me away for a long time now. But times like these do bring out the worst in people right?" Latrezz' mouth hung wide open in disbelief. "Excuse me for bein' rude. They call me Wet or just dub for short."

"Latrezz," It was Latrezz speaking but Wet's voice. He looked over at Wet who cheesed back at him, revealing razor sharp teeth.

"The pleasures all mines homie. I feel like gettin into some shit." Wet said as Latrezz handed him the wet daddy.

"Like what?" Latrezz asked.

"I don't know yet. Mob with me homie." Wet started out the door with Latrezz in toe.

CHAPTER 9

Detective Walker pulled up to Rodney's house and parked just as the teenager used crutches to limp on the porch. Walker approached the young man with a pen and note pad in his hands. "What happened?" He asked.

"What happened when?" Rodney responded calmly.

Walker's face turned red as he became agitated. "Look motherfucker, I don't have time for games. I'm here to help you out. So tell me who shot you!"

Rodney knew who Walker was and why he was there. Even though he was the victim he didn't want to be labeled a snitch. "I don't know I didn't see them."

"Who would want to hurt you?" Walker asked.

Rodney shrugged his shoulders. "I don't know I stay out of trouble."

Walker smirked, "Yea right. Who were you with?"

"I was alone." the teen insisted.

"Alone huh?" Walker looked him up and down. He didn't miss the black beenie Rodney sported that had the letter "A" on the front.

"Yep" Rodney replied.

"Nice hat motherfucker!" Walker stormed back to his vehicle and drove away. LIke most cops, he hated black people and it really got under his skin when they didn't do what he wanted. He rode away cursing. Rodney watched the detective's car dissappear down the street. Once Walker was out of sight, Rodney struggled down the stairs with his crutches.

Latrezz and Wet turned the corner onto Rodney's street. "Look there go one right there." Wet pointed in Rodney's direction.

"Yea but he a kid though and he look hurt." Latrezz reasoned.

"How you think he got that way?" Wet asked coldly.

Rodney made eye contact with Latrezz and turned around. He moved as expeditiously as he could, manueuvering the awkaward crutches for an unsteady balance. Wet ran at full speed and kicked Rodney in the leg, causing him to fall to the ground. He fell to the pavement groaning loudly as he clutched his knee. Wet picked up one of Rodney's crutches and used it to repeatedly strike his injured leg.

"Come on man! I didn't kill none of yo' homies. I just got caught in the crossfire." Rodney pleaded between groans. Latrezz walked closer to Rodney and Wet. HIs bone chilling gaze pierced the bloody and bruised teenager's soul.

Wet handed the crutch to Latrezz and chuckled. "Here homie, show him what's up with the Kill."

Rodney held his hands out in a pleading gesture. "Please Nut don't kill me! Randall, Stevie and One Shot the ones who killed Taz and Cliff, now their lookin for you. They be at One Shot crib off 9th and Going! PLEASE NUT!"

Latrezz raced down the street as fast as he could. No matter how fast he ran, he could still hear Wet's chilling voice in his ear. "It's time for a 187 we about to get them mothafuckas!"

"Naw man. Its too many people outside right now. I'd rather stake 'em out and then catch em slippin. Do it much worse you feel me." Latrezz said, still sprinting down the street.

Latrezz stopped running, all he could see was Wet's angry face. "What mothafucka! You know where the mothafuckas is at right now and you not down to do this shit?!"

"Hold up Killa Gang!!! I put in work like I was gettin paid for it. Everybody on the North East side know what's up wit O.G. Nut! One of the homies that put this Killingsworth Shit on the map!" Latrezz exclaimed.

Wet smiled. "So Nut is still on the set. I had forgot for a second. Lets do this shit!"

"I'm not about to go do that hot shit. You see how easy they little homie gave them mothafuckas up. If they come up dead right now stick a fork in me too!" Latrezz reasoned.

The grotesque clown was fuming, Latrezz was spooked as he felt the clown getting heated. He took off again. Wet's amplified voice carried through what felt like the whole universe. "What you tellin' me you not down for yo' family?"

Taz appeared in the middle of the street. "Nut!" he called out faintly. Latrezz stopped racing. He couldn't help the beast like panting sounds he made as he came to a halt.

Wet placed his hand on Latrezz' shoulder. "Cliff aint never bothered nobody."

Cliff appeared on the other end of the street waiving.

"CLIFF!..... CLIFF!" Latrezz hollered at the top of his lungs. A shower of tears fell from Latrezz' eyes.

"Where are you goin?" Cliff echoed faintly.

"CLIFF!" Latrezz called out again. He bolted down the street to Cliff. Latrezz hugged his nephew as tight as he could. He let go then stepped back to look at Cliff. "Nephew? I thought you was dead."

"Where are you goin?" Cliff asked again.

Wet swayed from side to side while circling Latrezz and Cliff. Wet whispered "9th & Going."

"Come on Unk. I know a short cut." Cliff said as he turned to run. The street became a forest full of tall grass and trees. Cliff turned around and motioned Latrezz to follow then disappeared into the grass. Latrezz disappeared into the grass behind his nephew. After swimming past a tall blade of grass, Latrezz found himself running behind his nephew on the St. Johns Bridge.

Latrezz cried and laughed at the same time. "You don't even look that bad. Let me see where they hit you at."

Cliff stopped in his tracks and began to lift his shirt. "Check this out."

At that moment Latrezz snapped back to reality. He found himself standing in his Mother's front yard. He appeared to be in a hazy daze as tears fell from his bloodshot red eyes. Mrs. Tillman stood directly in front of her son without him even noticing. The blood on his shoe was enough of a narrative for Latrezz' Mother to know what he'd been up to. "Where you goin?" Mrs. Tillman asked.

"9th & Going" He replied.

"9th & Going? What's over there Latrezz?" She questioned.

Latrezz began to mumble, he appeared confused. "Naw cuz me and Wet was goin that way-"

"Who?" Mrs. Tillman cut him off. "Are you hangin with them fools again?"

"Naw," Latrezz felt lost. "but I was goin for Cliff. I-"

Mrs. Tillman began crying. "Boy I done had enough for today now. I done already lost two. My heart cant take no more you hear me?!"

"Naw but Cliff and Taz..." Latrezz looked around the

block. Neighbors stared from their windows. Latrezz turned back to face his Mother. He cried out as he pointed, "Cliff…. Cliff and Taz was just right here."

Mrs. Tillman opened her arms and hugged Latrezz. He wept in her arms. "Come on baby you need some rest." She lead him into the house.

Mont slept in a dark room at his grandmother's house . On the night stand next to him was a bottle of prescription medicine and his phone. As the phone vibrated Mont opened his eyes. As he reached for his phone, he could feel all of the thick badges across his sore body. It was Baby Stomp. He hadn't seen him since the night of the party and wasn't anxious to hang out. He felt Baby Stomp was in it for the fame but not ready to go to war for the gang.

When Mont entered the living room he found his Mother and Grandmother in tears consoling each other at the dining room table. He limped through using the cumbersome crutches the doctor had given him. Retha wiped her eyes as she turned toward Mont.

"Hey baby boy. How you feelin?" Retha asked. Mont shrugged his shoulders.

"I know you feel blessed. You almost lost your life, you got to give an honor to GOD." Mrs. Tillman spoke up.

Mont's voice cracked as he spoke. "What about uncle Taz? What about my little brother? Why did Cliff have to die Grandma? "

"You know I ask myself the same thing. Why did he have to die? Why is it that black boys all across the United States go around killin' each other? Aint got a pot to piss in

129

but got the nerve to go out and kill somebody!" Mrs. Tillman wept hard. Her hands flew in the air, "Lord Jesus help me!"

Latrezz entered the room wearing house shoes and a tank top. "What you doin' up? I thought you supposed to be on bed rest?"

"Naw fuck that-" Mont snapped.

"Boy you better watch that mouth. I don't care what's goin on! All this silly gang shit got you thinkin' you bad. Who you gon hurt boy? Walkin' around here lookin like a damn flamingo! Now apologize." Mrs. Tillman scolded.

Mont dropped his head. "Sorry for cussing in your house Grandma."

"I'm not the only one in the room boy." Ms. Tillman added.

"Sorry Mama." Mont said softly as he looked to the ground.

"Did you forget about the person you was talkin to?" Latrezz spoke up.

Mont had a confused look on his face. "I cuss in front of you all the time."

"Not in my house you don't." Mrs. Tillman reminded her grandson.

"Maybe that's the problem." Retha added.

"Aight sorry man." Mont knew that his uncle was just toying with him in an attempt to make him laugh, however he was numb to humor.

Latrezz opened a closet and pulled hoody out then tossed it to Mont.
Mont caught the hoody then put it on. "Come on." he directed his nephew.

Retha jumped up. "No nu-uh. Where you takin my baby?"

"I got a spot for him to stay out the way. Y'all can come to. No tellin' when somebody gon come back shootin'." Latrezz informed his sister.

"I aint worried the LORD protects me." Mrs. Tillman responded.

"I aint leavin' either." Mont didn't want to feel like he was running.

Retha knew exactly what her son was thinking, she could hear the anger in his voice. "On second thought take this boy with you."

Mont followed Latrezz to the door. Latrezz opened it and let Mont walk pass. "Flamingo lookin' mothafucka." Latrezz stung his nephew under his breath.

Kisha couldn't stand to stay at home so she went to stay with her sister. She had left the keys to Latrezz. Latrezz took the opportunity to move his nephew in. Mont laid on the couch in the corner of the room as Latrezz pulled out a cigarette that he had dipped earlier.

Mont sat up. "Is that a cancer stick?"

Latrezz stopped in his tracks. He glanced down at the cigarette, then looked at Mont and shrugged his shoulders. "Stress'll make you do all kinds of new shit nephew." Latrezz said as he exited the room. Mont shook his head.

Latrezz stepped into the dark back yard and slowly lit the cigarette. He took a deep drag. HIs eyes became illuminated as he exhaled. He coughed violently causing him to hack up a thick loogy of mucus and saliva.

"Nut... Nut..." Wet's voice echoed in Latrezz' ear. Latrezz looked in every direction. "You's a nutty mothafucka mayne!" Wet's bass filled voice rumbled.

"So what's up are we ridin' tonight or what?" Latrezz asked.

Wet walked out of a shadow. He now stood the same height as Latrezz. His eyes gleamed red and his diabolical grin stretched across his whole face. "Oh so now you ready to put in some work homie?"

Latrezz took three hard drags off of his cigarette then tossed it away. "Let's do this shit."

"I go for blood." Wet smirked revealing his jagged piss yellow teeth.

"Me too." Latrezz replied.

Wet pulled a damp blunt out of his puffy red afro. A chilling chuckle escaped his mouth, as he held the blunt toward Latrezz. "Smoke this shit. Its gon make us stronger."

Latrezz took the blunt and held it to his lips. "Give me a light homie." As he lit the blunt Wet's eyes burned brighter. Flames appeared in the reflection of his pupils. Latrezz took a long drag off of the blunt then exhaled a dense cloud of smoke.

Meanwhile, One Shot, Stevie and Randall bent corners in search of a rival. When they turned down a back street Randall noticed a group of young men huddled on the corner. "Slow down cuddy." Randall spoke up. The white Entrepid crept down the dark street.

"Hand me the Mac, Stevie," Randall recognized Baby Stomp's car parked near the group. Stomp himself was across town with Cookie's cousin Nicole, he had her pick him up in the hood earlier that day. Stevie pulled the Mac-11 from under his seat then handed it to Randall who was sitting in the seat behind him. Randall cocked the bulky gun and exited the vehicle.

One of the young men in the group of Killingswoth Gangsters, tapped his comrade on the shoulder. "Look," He cautioned.

Randall paced toward the group with the large Mac-11 in his hand. He aimed at the crowd, then let off. BANG- BANG- TTTRRRATTT!!! Two of the men collapsed While the third man pulled a gun out of his pocket and returnd fire. POP POP POP.

"Fuck!" Randall yelled out as his gun jammed. A speeding bullet hit the top of his hat, knocking it to the ground. One Shot hopped out and immediately opened fire. BANG BANG BANG. The third man lost his balance. When he stumbled back to his feet, One Shot put the barrel of his gun to the young man's head forehead. POP! The man's lifeless body collapsed.

"That's how you lay a mothafucka down on the set." One Shot said as he threw his set up. He and Randall ran back to One Shot's car and stabbed out. Two of the young men from Killingsworth lie in the street slumped in a puddle of blood. The last of the men crawled away very slowly.

Up the street, Mont and his homies congregrated in Big Sherm's basement. Mont sat on the couch with his phone to his ear. Latrezz entered the basement.

"What?!" Mont jumped up then sat back down, still in pain from his injuries. He looked toward his uncle. "Uncle 'Trezz! Baby Squirrel and Knuckles just got killed."

"What?! Who is that?" Latrezz asked.

"Baby Stomp," He replied.

"Let me see the phone." Latrezz reached for the cell

phone. "What's happenin' Killa Gang?"

"One Shot and them came through blastin. We got two more dead homies." Baby Stomp replied.

"Meet me at the spot." Latrezz said then hung up the phone. Mont climbed to his feet. "What you doin' nephew?" Latrezz asked.

"I'm ridin' too. Fuck that!" Mont declared.

"Naw you might get hurt." What Latrezz feared the most was losing Lamont in the same fashion he lost Taz and Cliff.

"They can't hurt me, I died with my little brother." Cliff stated coldly. Latrezz and Mont exchanged a cold stare. They had both just lost a brother and bestfriend, they shared the same pain and blood.

Wet, standing almost 6'5, walked into the room rolling a blunt. "Let the little nigga roll."

"Damn nephew! Come on man." Latrezz welcomed his nephew to the mission. Mont limped toward the door behind his uncle.

When they pulled up to Farragut Park, Big Sherm and Black stood surrounded by young black men in dark clothing. Mont slowly limped toward the circle. Latrezz walked behind him the same way a bodyguard would walk behind the president. The group of men looked toward Latrezz and Mont walking through the shadows.

"That's just Mont and Nut." Sherm announced.

"What's up y'all," Mont greeted his homies.

"What's up Mont. What you doin out here?" Black questioned.

"Them mothafuckas missed!" Mont answered.

Big Sherm chuckled in his deep husky voice. "Mont hard aint he? Should have been my deuce."

"Taz and Nut my G's. No disrespect but them is the only names that I'm carryin'." Mont declared so the whole set could hear. Latrezz looked up toward his nephew, he was caught off guard that Mont still idolized him.

Big Sherm twisted his face then smiled. He let out a delayed chuckle. "Right, right. I hear you mayne."

"Fuck the small talk. Its time to do this shit." Latrezz announced as he turned toward his car with his nephew in toe.

"Nut," Big Sherm called out. Latrezz and Mont both turned around.

"What's up?" Latrezz asked.

"Let me holla at you real quick." Sherm replied. Latrezz and Big Sherm stood away from the group near a large tree. Sherm leaned in. "How that Wet been treatin' you?"

"That shit was cool," Latrezz responded. He didn't want to reveal the things he had seen since indulging in the drug.

Big Sherm examined him closely, then handed him a small jar. "Here mayne let's tear these mothafuckas up." Wet stood in the shadows in the distance. His eyes burned fiery red.

Latrezz drove with his nephew in the front street through the neighborhood. They could feel the bass from the music deep in their chests. Their faces were emotionless. Behind them Big Sherm drove with Black in the front seat and another young man in the back. There was two blunts in rotation, causing the inside of their car to be foggy. A few more cars filled with Killingsworth Gangsters all crept toward One Shot's house.

Inside the basemnt, several of the Alberta Gangsters

sat around smoking, drinking and planning out their next hit. Stevie lifted weights while his brother loaded an assault rifle. Randall shot dice on the floor with a group of teenaged members. There is a fresh tattoo that read "187" on Randall's trigger finger.

Rodney struggled to his feet with the assistance of his crutches. The badly battered young man looked toward JR who stood near him. "That mothafucka Nut is crazy bro. Somebody need to kill that mothafucka quick!"

"Where was yo' burner at when he ran up on you?" JR asked.

"I had just stepped out to get some fresh air." he replied.

"What that mean? Its funk season and you just got popped. You got to stay ready out here." JR lectured his friend.

"Yea I got something for him." Rodney said in an attempt to hide his fear.

Outside Latrezz parked at the corner while another car slowly drove past One Shot's house. Several young men emerged from the shadows. Black and Big Sherm stood near the front window pointing their guns inside. They nod to each other then began shooting into the house. Every one in the basement ducked and clutched their guns. One Shot bolted toward the door carrying his assault rifle.

Three young black men wearing dark clothing emerged from One Shot's backyard. Black shot one of the men in the shoulder. The lightning fast slug spun the man around. A stampede of people ran up the street, away from the gun fight.

Mont spotted a stocky dark skinned man in the crowd then let off two shots from Latrezz' car. "Stevie!" Mont blurted out. Latrezz looked toward his nephew. Mont pointed down the street. "There he go unk. Lets get him!"

Big Sherm and Black run to Big Sherm's car. "We got to shake. Lets go!" They hopped in and sped away. Latrezz' car sped off in the opposite direction. One Shot emerged into the middle of the street with the long assault rifle in his hand. He aimed and shot down the street. Tat-tat-tat-tat-tat. A shower of bullets shatter both the front and back windows of Big Sherm's car. Black's shirt was drenched in blood. He clutched his stomach as he busted shots from the passenger window.

Big Sherm ducked his head as he steered the driving wheel violently. "FUCK!" Big Sherm exclaimed.

Black groaned loadly. "Mothafuckas!!!" he cursed them.

Big Sherm's car sped pass a police car that happened to be parked in an alley. The police car's sirens flashed and began to sound off. The patrol car sped out of the alley behind Big Sherm's car. Black was slumped over, passed out from losing too much blood. Big Sherm sweated profusely. The adrenalin in his veins didn't allow him to notice the gushing wound on his right shoulder.

"Pull over! You can't get away. We know who you are. This is your last warning to pull over." The sound of the police intercom filled the street.

"Damn what in the fuck am I goin to do?!" Big Sherm's question went unanswered. He looked over and saw Black slumped over in the passenger seat.

Over a dozen police cars with their sirens on filled the street. A total of seventeen offiicers surrounded Big Sherm's car with their weapons drawn. "Dont move or I'll blow your fucking head off!!!" One of the officers threatened.

Big Sherm held is his chubby hands in the air, each

finger fatter than a hot dog. "Aight, I ain't runnin'." The officers barbously heaved Big Sherm out of the car and sat him on the curb with his hands cuffed behind his back. He looked over his shoulder as Black was placed in the back of an ambualance. Detective Walker walked up with a note pad in his hand.

"You want to tell me what the fuck is goin on here?" Walker asked.

"Some random fools started bustin' on us. I'm tryin' to get my homie to the hospital. He about to bleed to death. What's up why hasn't the ambulance left yet?" Big Sherm questioned.

"We have witnesses saying that you were the aggressor in a shooting on 9th & Going." Walker informed him.

"Fuck all that. Get my homie to a hospital then we can talk." Big Sherm responded.

Walker laughed insensitively. "What homie?"

A few blocks away, Latrezz' eyes screamed fury as he sped through the rain soaked streets.

"Look there they go right there." Mont pointed at a group of young men huddled in the shadows at Irving Park.

"Stay over here either in the car or in the bushes. If any of them niggas come yo' way blast on 'em." Latrezz ordered.

"I want Stevie!" Mont insisted making eye contact with his uncle.

"I won't kill him." Latrezz promised his nephew.

Latrezz stealthily crept through the park. In his left hand he held a burning sherm stick, in his right was a large gun. The more drags he took off of the blunt, the foggier the whole park became.

Wet materialized in the dense fog. He now stood nearly a burly 7 feet tall. The pale clown's sinister face twisted into an evil sneer, his eyes smoldered neon red. He let out a deep chuckle. "Let's do this shit,"

Latrezz aimed his gun then fired. One of the men collapsed, the rest of the crowd dispersed. Two of the men ran toward the exit of the park, directly into Latrezz' trap. Mont stepped out of the bushes and fired his gun rapidly. BANG BANG BANG BANG. Both of the men were cut down by Mont's furious ambush. He slowly approached the two injured men.

Another Alberta Gang member stopped in his tracks after running into what he thought was a tree. Wet viciously back hand slapped the man, sending him flying backwards. He grabbed another man by his throat then violently choke slammed him. Wet held the man by his feet and swung him in a circle. When he let the man go his body flew into the air. Wet aimed his big yellow revolver at the flying man. BANG! BANG! BANG! Two bullets pierced the man's face. Some how his foot got caught in the net of the basket ball hoop, leaving him hanging upside down. Warm blood drained out of his wounds onto the court as his eyes rolled to the back of his head.

A stocky man slowly crawled through the park. Latrezz walked closely behind him. "Heard you was lookin' for me," Latrezz said before kicking the injured man in the ribs. "Well you found the Nutty nigga, what's up?!"

The stocky man turned over. Sweat dripped off of his face onto his blood drenched, grass stained clothes. "Nut! Please don't kill me Nut!"

"You thought you could just get away with that shit Stev-"

The man cut Latrezz off. "Naw man, Stevie and them still back there. I aint Stevie. Please don't kill me! I just got put on the set when I was on lock down. I just came home today. Cliff was my homie,"

Wet violently stomped on the man's face several times. All Latrezz could hear was cracking and squishing sounds. Blood and brains splattered in every direction. Wet chuckled as he stepped back. When Wet stopped stomping, the stocky man's head was missing. There was a large puddle of blood above his shoulders. In the blood floated guts and bone fragments. Wet laughed obnoxiously.

"Mothafucka!" Mont's eyes grew wide as he looked out of the window.

Latrezz drove in silence as Mont slowly lit a blunt. "What the fuck uncle Trezz. You was supposed to save Stevie for me."

"That wasn't Stevie. He was still in there. I knew I should've left you at home. I would've stayed and killed all of them mothafuckas. Now they know their spot is hot." Latrezz said, he was more upset with himself for not going with his first judgment. Mont dropped his head to his chest.

Latrezz' cell phone started ringing, it was Sandy. He held the phone to his ear. "Hello."

Sandy sat with Mrs. TIllman and Retha watching television. "Breaking News." flashed across the screen as it cut to One Shot's house. Retha nervously smoked a cigarette gazing into space.

"Where are you baby?" Sandy asked.

"I'm around what's up?" Latrezz answered.

"When are you coming home? I'm at your Mom's house watching the news. They said that four shootings have left ten people dead and thirteen wounded." Mont could hear the fear in his women's voice.

"Im okay. I'll be by there in a minute." He assured his woman.

"Okay. Be safe." she replied.

Latrezz hung his phone up and looked over to his nephew. "So you Little Nut huh?"

"Everybody say that I act just like you. I put in the work and I earned the name." Mont insisted.

"But would you lay your life down for this Killingsworth shit?" Latrezz took a deep drag.

"Not for the street itself, but for my family and respect I would." Mont took a deep breath. "Shit look at me Unk, I already got one foot in the grave over this shit!"

"I know where they at." Latrezz informed his nephew as his phone began to ring again. Latrezz passed Mont the blunt. "Yea?"

On the other end of the line, Big Sherm finally had the opportunity to use the phone. Two young inmates in the background talked amongst themselves as they looked in his direction.

"Nut this Sherm." He announced.

"Where you at?" Mont asked.

Big Sherm held the phone to his ear as he looked toward the two young men behind him. "I'm locked up I had my girl three-way you. It's not lookin that good for Black either."

Latrezz slapped the steering wheel. "FUCK!"

"Can you do my laundry for me?" Sherm asked.

"Enough said." Latrezz hung up the phone.

Toya sat crying with the phone to her ear. "What are we gon do Daddy?" she asked.

"Don't worry about nothin'. It's all about us and our future. I'll be home before you know it. Love you." Big Sherm assured his woman.

Toya could not fight back the tears, "Love you too."

Big Sherm hung up the phone and approached the two young men. They flashed the Alberta sign. Big Sherm's massives arm punched each of the men once in the face, crumbling both of the young men.

Latrezz and Mont roamed the hallways of Emanuel hospital. Latrezz wore blue scrubs with a hair net and a doctor mask as he pushed his nephew in a wheel chair. Mont kept a sturdy grip on the large duffle bag in his lap. "They had us down here. Go in that room on the right." Mont directed. Latrezz pushed the wheelchair into the room.

When they entered the room several beds were fiiled with young black men in them. Mont lit a blunt, then looked at it disqusted. "What the fuck is this?"

Latrezz looked down at his nephew. "Where did you get that from?"

"It was in your ashtray." Mont replied.

"Damn it Lamont! How many times I got to tell you not to take my shit with out askin." Latrezz scolded his nephew after realizing what had happened. Wet walked into the room dressed as a doctor with a surgical mask covering his face. His bright red hair peaked out of the hair net on his head. He chuckled obnoxiously as he fiddled with an extremely large needle.

"What the fuck?! Who the fuck is that?" Mont asked.

"I'm the O.G. homie. Been bringin hell to these streets for a long time." Wet answered him.

Mont pulled a gun out of the duffle bag. He aimed it at Wet and let off. BANG BANG BANG. Clifford materialized in Wet's place. The bullets pierced his body, the same as when he was killed. Mont jumped up and ran toward Clifford.

Cliff looked up from the floor, "Get out of here."

Tears poured out of Mont's eyes. "Bro, I didn't know that was you. What the hell?"

Wet stood at the head of one of the beds with a large axe in his hands. He cocked his massive arm back. "I'm on your side homie. See?" Wet went from bed to bed violently attacking the injured men with the axe.

In another area in the ICU, the only sounds in Black's room came from the vital monitors and life support machines that pumped oxygen and fluids into his motionless body. A doctor, holding a clip board stood at the door with a nurse.

"I think he'll pull through." The doctor announced.

Meanwhile, Big Sherm's forehead was covered in beads of sweat. The lights in the interrogation room baked the large man. He couldn't remember the last time he had went this long without eating, his stomach growled and rumbled. Detective Walker entered the room and placed a large slab of ribs on the table.

"So are you ready to talk fat boy?" Walker jested the massive man.

"About what?! Let me get some of them ribs you pasty mothafucka! You bullshittin." Big Sherm's thunderous voice carried. Walker's face turned red. He hated the sound of their voices.

"Well I need names. I need to know who's been doing the shootings around here. And I need to know what crazy motherfucker is lighting people on fire." Walker knew Big Sherm was deep in the game and hoped this would turn into convictions.

"What you think I'm about to snitch for a slab of ribs?" Big Sherm asked between smacking ribs.

"What do you want?" Walker asked.

Big Sherm paused, then looked Walker in the eyes. "To be free."

Walker folded his arms. "Give me a case. Your boy is done, but you still have a chance." Walker prayed that Latrezz' name came out of Sherm's mouth.

"I was only there to pick Black up…" Big Sherm was under the impression that Black wouldn't make it, so he implicated his friend to save himself.

CHAPTER 10

The morning of Taz and Cliff's funeral was typical for a Portland winter. The city was wet, muggy and gray. Even non-affiliates could feel the murder and tension in the air. Katie drove in silence as Mont and Latrezz passed blunts back and forth. They were all dressed in dark dress clothing for the mournful occasion.

"I'm sorry about your loss. Cliff was so cool." Katie expressed her empathy.

"Well I appreciate you bein here." Latrezz responded.

"No problem." She said.

"What's been goin on at school?" Latrezz hadn't been to school or work in almost three weekks, he was too busy taking care of *Nut's* business.

Katie took a long drag off the blunt, then twirled her dreads. "The usual, Professor Thomas sends his regards. What about your job dude?"

"I'm supposed to go in there next week for a drug test. You got any ideas?" Latrezz knew that once his employer saw the PCP in his system that he wouldn't have a chance.

"I got some stuff for you but you would have to be sober for at least five days before taking it. For heavy drugs at least seven days." She advised her friend. "One summer me and a bunch of my friends spent the weekend at a cabin on Mt. Hood. We experimented with all types of stuff. Shrooms, acid, coke, ice..."

"Damn y'all was lit like a muthafucka huh?!" Mont was astonished to hear Katie talk about using hardcore drugs so casually.

Katie shrugged her shoulders. "It's only bad if you get caught man. I took a U.A. a week later and passed."

"What job was that?" Mont inquired.

"Job?" She shook her head, "I was on probation!"

"Hell naw!" Mont thought it was implausible that the harmless hipppy had a rap sheet. "Where you find this white girl unk? She low key with the shit."

Katie giggled, Mont felt laughter rumbling through every wound in his body. It was the first time he'd reallly laughed since his brother died. Latrezz found the conversation humerous as well. However, his face remained frozen in a daze as he gazed out the window.

Inside the church, the choir wore black gowns and sang slow hymns. Twelve young men wearing dark suits, white gloves and sunglasses pushed the two caskets to the front of the church. The sorrowful occasion brought out gangmembers who hadn't been seen in years, hood rats and childhood associates.

Mrs. Tillman and Retha sat in the front pew, crying hysterically. Lamont sat next to his Mother, a stream of tears rolled from under the dark shades onto his face. Latrezz sat in between Ms. TIllman and Sandy. Sandy clutched Latrezz' hand as she stared into his eyes.

Mont turned his head toward the pews behind him. He spotted Juan sitting near the back of the church next to another Mexican man. They were dressed in silk shirts with dark shades on. Juan nodded his head, Mont nodded back. Mont also noticed Cookie and her cousins sitting in the back as well. He hadn't spoke to her ever since he checked himself out of the hospital. Once they made eye contact he quickly turned back around. He was embarassed to cry in front of her.

The teens in attendance directed their attention toward the neatly dressed man walking to the front of the church. He wore an expensive leather jacket, a thick gold herring bone and had gold rings on almost every finger.

"Look," Baby Stomp nudged the teen next to him. "That's Prescott Mont."

Lamont had not seen his father in almost five years. The sound of his dad's deep voice only agitated the young man. "What's up Junior?"

Lamont looked up and became more angry at the man who looked almost identical to him and his late brother. "My name aint no mothafuckin' Junior! I'm Lil' Nut from Killingsworth Street!"

Mrs. Tillman stopped sobbing and grabbed her Grandson's arm. "Don't use that kind of language in the house of the Lord you hear me boy?!"

Mont nodded then stood to his feet. He briefly looked his father up and down, then stormed out of the sanctuary. Latrezz turned his head toward his nephews' father. Prescott Mont gave a head nod and held his hand out. Latrezz looked at Prescott Mont in disgust and followed his nephew out of the sanctuary.

"Where the hell yo' sorry ass been at Lamont?" Retha's voice shrieked through the church. "Left me to raise these boys by myself and now look what happened!"

"How you gon' blame this on me. I would've never had my boys out here bangin'. He obviously followin' his uncles' example not mines!" Prescott Mont snapped.

Retha stood to her feet and got in Prescott Mont's face. "What example did you set huh?" She pointed her finger in his face. "When the last time you seen these boys? You aint shit but a washed up popcorn pimp! Don't you ever speak on my brothers, deadbeat MOTHAFUCKA!"

"Oh, its like that huh," Presscott Mont didn't have a rebuttle.

"Its the truth." Mrs. Tillman chimed in.

Meanwhile, One Shot, Stevie and Randall were still on a mission. They slowly cruised the streets near the church.

"That shit the other night was fucked up. It's time to put it all on the line now." Stevie said. The trio was so focused on catching another body that they didn't notice Walker's car following behind them.

Back inside the church, the preacher stood in the pulpit sweating with a microphone in his hand. He paced back and forth from the pulpit to the altar, at times looking at the two lifeless bodies in front of him as he delivered his sermon.

"These were good boys. Children of GOD! But ya see, ya see GOD works in mysterious ways. And when evil is present there aint no tellin how things are going to end up. So to all of you young boys out there thinking about joining a gang... Or if you're already in a gang... " The preacher paused and surveyed the crowd. "Give your life to God. Aint no Gang deeper than the Lord's you understand me...." His words were followed by several "Amens" and applause from the pews.

Outside, One Shot pulled over on the corner of the block. He finally noticed Walker's car pulling over behind him. One Shot clutched his gun.

"I'm not goin back to jail until Nut and Mont are dead." Stevie declared. Randall cocked his gun.

Detective Walker walked up to One Shot's window. "Can you step out of the car for me sir?" One Shot's eyes were ice cold as he looked toward the red faced detective.

Inside the church several grieving people marched to the alter to give their final farewells. BANG! BANG! BANG! The crowd began to scatter and duck at the sound of distant gun shots. Some young men reached into their pockets.

"Okay I need every body to stay calm and to duck!" The preacher yelled out before exiting the room through a door behind the choir stand. A few people tried to follow, however he pulled the door closed behind him.

Mont jumped up and ran out of the church, pistol in hand. Latrezz, Juan and several other young men followed. In the chaotic frenzy that was taking place, no one noticed Mrs. Tillman kneeling at the altar. She was only focused on GOD as she prayed over her son and grandson.

Outside, Walker ducked behind a trash can with a gun in his hand. He bled from his leg. Randall was face down on the side walk with his hands cuffed behind his back. One Shot was stretched out on the sidewalk bleeding and gasping for breath.

Stevie ducked behind One Shot's car. He busted shots over the car at Walker. BANG BANG BANG BANG!!!

Mont exited the church with his gun drawn. He immediately fired in Stevie's direction. The crowd of gangsters rushed out of the church behind Mont. Stevie fired into the crowd striking the older Mexican man who came with Juan.

Mont returned fire in Stevie's direction. Two bullets

SMACKED Stevie in the chest. The stocky man stumbled to the ground. His gun fell from his grasp as blood oozed onto the ground from under him.

Mont stood over One Shot and aimed at point blank range. BANG! The lightning fast bullet pierced the back of One Shot's head. Walker crawled to his knees as he pointed his gun at Mont's back. Latrezz, out of nowhere, violently kicked Detective Walker in the face knocking him unconscious. Latrezz violently stomped Walker then pulled out his gun and aimed it at Randall. Sandy stood in front of the gun crying.

"Move Sandy!" He demanded.

"Don't you see? If you do this you're going to jail for a long time. I can't raise this baby on my own." She pleaded, sobbing.

Latrezz slightly lowerd his gun. He looked Sandy in the eyes. Tears of frustration rolled down his cheeks.

"Lets just go please." Sandy pleaded. As the sound of approaching sirens grew louder, she pulled Latrezz away.

Police cars emerged onto the block. Several officers pepper sprayed the crowd and used their tasers on random people. Five officers participated in detaining Mont. They violently shoved the injured teen onto the ground. While two of them forced his hands behind his back, an obese white officer with a bald head and a pepper red face, planted his knee on the back of Mont's head.

Retha ran toward Mont. "He's just a boy, don't man handle him like that!" An officer pepper sprayed Retha, stopping her in her tracks. She coughed violently and gasped for air.

Two officers pushed Randall into the back of a police car. Randall looked out of the window making eye contact with Mont. Mont returned a sinister grin to his rival.

Later at the police station, Walker's face was severely bruised. He paced back and forth limping. Mont sat at the interrogation table smirking. He found the detective's injuries to be comical.

"Look I can get you back on the streets by the time you're twenty one. All I need is your testimony tellin' me who's behind all of the gruesome murders that occurred. I don't care about the shootings." Walker insisted.

"Were you going to kill me?" Mont asked.

Detective Walker was baffled at the question. He didn't understand how Mont could've seen him. "Who told you that? Who kicked me? Was it Latrezz?"

Mont laughed obnoxiously. "Naw mothafucka. Send me to my cell this shit is over!"

With the help of his family, Latrezz was able to regain control of his life. He became full time at his job and focused more on his education. He made every Doctor's appointment and parenting class Sandy had scheduled and was able be there when his son was born. Mont wasn't so lucky. He still had no idea that Cookie was pregnant and he faced up to life in prison if he lost in court. Because of Big Sherm's cop out, Black woke up to a secret indictment. They joined Nacho in the county jail.

Portland had become so filthy that even the police

officers faced criminal charges. The F.B.I. and Internal Affairs were conducting investigations on the department after several complaints regarding "questionable incidents" flooded the governor's office. Allegations from the community included tampering with evidencs, extortion and even attempted murder. Walker was accused of racial profiling, harrassment and fifth degree manslaughter. Mont's defense argued that One Shot died from injuries sustained at the hands of Walker. Somehow, the story made national news and civil rights groups began to campaign for indicting the detective, which led to the department wide investigation.

On the streets, things died down after a few months. Big Sherm fell off the radar. When the smoke cleared, Baby Stomp had finessed himself into a shot caller for to the little homies from Killingsworth Street. In Salem, Juan and the 541 gang was in a heated war with their rival "Tha Otha Side." They had not forgot about the loss they took to the Alberta Street gang. JR fled to Las Vegas, fearing that he would soon be dead or in jail if he stayed in town. Once Cookie's father learned she was pregnant, he moved his family back to Oklahoma.

Mont layed on his bunk looking at the ceiling. All he could think about was Taz and Cliff. The highlight of his day was when he got to speak to his surviving uncle on the phone. Retha and Mrs. Tillman visited him every sunday. They usually played cards and talked about the good old days. This was the closest he felt to his Mother in years, ironically.

Today however was a Tuesday, which meant no visit and Latrezz was at school or work most of the day. Lamont closed his eyes and pictured Cookie's pretty brown skin in front of him. He wondered how she was doing and was optimistic about somehow contacting her.

Lamont opened his eyes when he heard the sound of the trustee's rusty cart squeeling down the corrider. When the cart pulled up to his cell he was in disbellief once he noticed the gruesome pale clown dressed in inmate clothing. He slid an envelope through the opening of the cell door. Mont picked up the envelope and opened it revealing a sherm stick. Every night after the lights went out Wet returned with another. The creepy chuckling haunted him every night.

GLOSSARY

Jug/ Jugging (pg 5)- bartering

Bail (page 6)- rhythmic strut.

Off Brand (page 10)- enemy, rival

Fade (Page 11)- fist fight

Rocked Off (Page 12)- to strike the first blow

Thang (Page 12)- firearm

Dodi (PG 12)- marijuana

Bomb (PG 13)- good weed

Soft Legs (PG 13)- female, woman

Bend Corners (PG 13)- to travel by automobile

Put Bid In (PG 15)- Show romantic interest

Pasty (PG 15)- European American

Cup Cake (PG 16)- to show an excessive amount of fondness

Mixed in (PG 19)- Initiated via physical combat, usually verse multiple people

Tap In (PG 21)- Touch Basis

Cracking (PG 24)- Having a good time

Dummy Mission (PG 29)- To execute a plan that's sure to fail

Sellling Wolf Tickets (PG 34)- to lie

Thirsty (PG 36)- Lustful

Stuffer (PG 36)- An unreliable vehicle

Vikes (PG 41)- Vicodin

Kush Coma (PG 51)- Sleep or very sluggish as result of smoking Kush weed

Hitting Licks (51)- Providing goods or services for money

Nascar (PG 58)- Cocaine

Gangbang Groupie (PG 87)- Woman who dates and associates herself with gangbangers

Swap (PG 95)- Bad Weed

Pocket Rocket (PG 108)- smaller pistol

Smash Off (PG 109)- speed away

ABOUT THE AUTHOR

T.M. McCauley is a film maker who grew up in North East Portland which inspired his stories and flavor. Although troubled as a teen, McCauley always aspired to make use of his creativity. He sharpened his writing skills while attending Jefferson High School and Clark Atlanta Unversity. For more content visit www.headupentertainment.com